Laia put her hand on his bare chest.

Exactly as she'd wanted to the other day.

Dax's eyes flared. He put his hand over hers. But he didn't pull hers away.

His skin was warm. Still damp from the sea. She could feel his heart. Strong and steady. Maybe a little fast. Like hers. His hand felt huge enveloping hers.

"Laia, what are you doing?"

Her eyes fell to his mouth. It wasn't thin anymore. It was lush and full. She frowned, her mind not able to let go of the strand of thought she'd just been picking at in spite of Dax's warnings. She asked, "What happened to make your brother give you a life of freedom?"

She looked up as something occurred to her. He saw it in her eyes and before she could say another word, Dax had snaked his free hand under her wet hair and around to the back of her neck, and then his mouth was on hers, and Laia ___'t have any thoughts in her head anymore. ___use they were incinerated by the fire.

Hot Winter Escapes

Sun, snow and sexy seductions...

Whether it's a trip to the Swiss Alps or a rendezvous on a gorgeous Hawaiian beach, warming up in front of the fire or basking in the sizzling sun, these billion-dollar getaways provide the perfect backdrops for even more scorching winter romances and passionately-ever-afters!

Escape to some winter sun in...

Bound by Her Baby Revelation by Cathy Williams

An Heir Made in Hawaii by Emmy Grayson

Claimed by the Crown Prince by Abby Green

One Forbidden Night in Paradise by Louise Fuller

And get cozy in these luxurious snowy hideaways...

A Nine-Month Deal with Her Husband
by Joss Wood

Snowbound with the Irresistible Sicilian
by Maya Blake

Undoing His Innocent Enemy
by Heidi Rice

In Bed with Her Billionaire Bodyguard
by Pippa Roscoe

All available now!

Abby Green

CLAIMED BY THE CROWN PRINCE

PRESENTS

HARLEQUIN®
PRESENTS™

Recycling programs for this product may not exist in your area.

ISBN-13: 978-1-335-59312-2

Claimed by the Crown Prince

Copyright © 2023 by Abby Green

For questions and comments about the quality of this book, please contact us at CustomerService@Harlequin.com.

Harlequin Enterprises ULC
22 Adelaide St. West, 41st Floor
Toronto, Ontario M5H 4E3, Canada
www.Harlequin.com

Printed in U.S.A.

Irish author **Abby Green** ended a very glamorous career in film and TV—which really consisted of a lot of standing in the rain outside actors' trailers—to pursue her love of romance. After she'd bombarded Harlequin with manuscripts, they kindly accepted one, and an author was born. She lives in Dublin, Ireland, and loves any excuse for distraction. Visit abby-green.com or email abbygreenauthor@gmail.com.

Books by Abby Green

Harlequin Presents

Bound by Her Shocking Secret
A Ring for the Spaniard's Revenge
His Housekeeper's Twin Baby Confession

Hot Summer Nights with a Billionaire

The Flaw in His Red-Hot Revenge

Jet-Set Billionaires

Their One-Night Rio Reunion

Passionately Ever After...

The Kiss She Claimed from the Greek

Princess Brides for Royal Brothers

Mistaken as His Royal Bride

Visit the Author Profile page
at Harlequin.com for more titles.

This is for the lovely country and people of Malaysia—I was lucky enough to work and live there for a few months a long time ago. KL, Penang, Langkawi, Ipoh...all hold very special places in my heart. It's a magical place and I hope everyone gets a chance to visit at least once.

CHAPTER ONE

HE'D FOUND HER. A sense of intense satisfaction rolled through Dax as he took a seat in the beach bar—on the far opposite corner to where the woman sat at a table alone, with her laptop in front of her and a big floppy sun hat covering most of her hair and features.

She might have been any number of travellers in this laid-back beach bar on the beautiful Malaysian island of Langkawi. It was a mecca for backpackers and sun worshippers, with its white sand beaches and glittering green waters.

But Dax knew she wasn't just any other traveller. And she certainly wasn't a backpacker. For a start, he noted the not exactly discreet security detail keeping watch over her. Two burly men who looked as if they were desperately trying to blend in and failing miserably.

Because the woman was Crown Princess Laia Sant Roman of Isla'Rosa, a small independent kingdom in the Mediterranean. A long way away from here.

She was a queen-in-waiting. Heiress to an ancient line of kings and queens who had battled to protect their modest rock in the sea. Dax knew her history and lineage well—because he was also not just a random traveller, in spite of his khaki cargo shorts and short-sleeved shirt.

He was the Crown Prince of Santanger, the neighbouring island kingdom and heir to his own throne, if anything happened to his brother the King and until his brother had heirs.

Which was where this woman came in. She'd been promised in marriage to his brother since she was born. A pact made by their fathers—the two late Kings—in order to ensure lasting peace and diplomacy in the region after hundreds of years of enmity and war.

But to say she was reluctant was an understatement. Dax had vague memories of her father visiting Santanger when he'd been younger, but Laia had only accompanied the King a couple of times. Dax remembered her as small and dark-haired, with wide eyes. A serious expression.

Since her father's death, she appeared to have turned avoiding his brother into an art form. And now, mere weeks before the wedding was due to take place, she'd flitted to south-east Asia.

She, unlike her security team, did fade into the crowd a little better. Especially for one so exceptionally beautiful.

Dax's insides clenched with an awareness that he desperately ignored.

Not welcome. Not appropriate.

But it was there nonetheless. And it had been there ever since they'd crossed paths one night in a club in Monaco over a year ago—his first time seeing her again since she was a young girl. Like Dax, Princess Laia had cultivated a reputation as a lover of socialising, earning her the moniker of The Party Princess.

Except, strangely enough, while Laia had been photographed at almost every 'it' social event in the past four years—most of which Dax himself had frequented—he'd never actually seen her in the flesh. Even though they'd both appeared in the papers in the days following the said events.

Dax had his suspicions as to why that was, but he'd never had the opportunity to say it to the Princess until he'd seen her at that event for the launch of one of the biggest motor races a year ago.

She'd been on the dance floor in a green silk strapless jumpsuit, with a silver belt around her slim waist. High-heeled sandals. Hair down around her shoulders. She'd looked like the beauties who'd used to grace the iconic Studio 54 club in New York in the seventies. Except she was far more beautiful.

She'd had her eyes closed and had looked as if she was in a world of her own. Dax had felt almost a little jealous of her absorption. He'd walked over to her, and as he'd approached—as if sensing him—her eyes had opened and she'd looked directly at him.

Her eyes were huge and almond-shaped and very green. Long lashes. Exquisite bone structure. Straight nose. Lush mouth. A classic beauty, of that there was no doubt. And Dax, who was a well-known connoisseur of women, had felt—such a cliché—as if he'd never seen true beauty until that moment. Her effect on him had been like a punch to the gut.

He hadn't been able to breathe. Literally hadn't been

able to find a breath for a long moment. She'd looked at him as if she'd never seen a man before. Eyes wide.

He'd seen her indicate to her security team that it was okay to let him approach. A subtle movement. The heaving crowd around them had disappeared. It had as if they were enclosed in an invisible bubble.

But then she'd blinked and, as if she'd come out of a trance, an expression of distaste had crossed her face. Dax would have sworn he'd felt a chill breeze skate over his skin. The temperature had definitely dropped a few degrees.

She'd made a small bow, but it had felt to him like a mockery. She'd looked at him.

'Crown Prince Dax of Santanger... What a pleasure to meet you in your favoured habitat.'

Dax had been surprised at the unmistakable scorn in her tone. After all, they'd never really met face to face, and she was promised in matrimony to his brother. She would become his family.

He'd felt compelled to respond with a bow of his own, saying, 'I could say the same of you, Your Highness. We seem to frequent all the same social events and yet you're as elusive as the Scarlet Pimpernel.'

She'd paled dramatically at that.

He'd frowned and put out his hand to steady her, 'Are you okay?'

Her arm had felt incredibly slim, yet strong, skin like warm silk. He'd had an impression of steeliness.

She'd pulled away from him, colour washing back into her cheeks. 'Don't touch me.'

Dax had lifted his hand in a gesture of appeasement, surprised at her vehemence. She'd looked at her security team then—another subtle movement—and Dax had found himself behind a solid wall of muscle as she'd left the dance floor.

He'd watched her leave, wondering what the hell had just happened. But he hadn't been alone for long.

'Hey, Prince Handsome, care to dance?'

Dax had torn his eyes from where Princess Laia had been fast retreating and looked down. A woman had come up beside him in a sparkling dress revealing more than it hid. Seeing her overly made-up face, and the very tell-tale glitter of synthetic substances in her unfocused eyes, he'd felt such a profound sense of ennui come over him that he'd walked straight out of the club—just in time to see a sleek chauffeur-driven SUV pull away from the kerb, followed by the recognisable security detail.

Dax had been eschewing his own security for some time by then, in spite of his brother's protests, for complicated reasons that went to the root of who he was and the burden of guilt he'd carried for years. Quite simply, he didn't deserve to be protected. He certainly wouldn't be responsible for someone putting their life ahead of his.

As he'd watched those vehicles disappear he'd felt, ridiculously, as if he'd just lost something. When he'd made it his life's purpose not to have much of an attachment to anything. Apart from his brother. It had been a long time since anyone else had made Dax *feel* anything. Not since the dark days of his mother's tragic death. A death he still held himself accountable for.

His emotions were rarely engaged now, and that was the way he liked it.

Even when he wanted a woman it was fleeting and quickly satisfied. But what had happened between him and Princess Laia had gone beyond mere *wanting*, although that had been there too.

But there had been nothing he could do about it because she was the one woman Dax couldn't touch.

She was promised to his brother.

Which was why he was here. In a rustic beach bar in Malaysia. To take her back to Santanger so she could fulfil her duty. Marry his brother and beget heirs.

A bilious knot formed in his gut at the thought of her with his brother. He chastised himself—she was beautiful and he couldn't have her. That was all it was. FOMO. He smiled mirthlessly at himself.

It was time to let his brother know he had found her and would be bringing her back.

Dax put his hand out to retrieve his phone from where he'd put it on the table but his hand found nothing. He looked down. There was an empty space where he'd laid it just moments before. He looked up, his eye catching a small Malaysian kid on the other side of the bar, who was handing Crown Princess Laia what looked like a phone.

His phone.

She smiled at the boy indulgently and handed him some *ringgit*. The boy skipped away, delighted with himself, counting the money. She slipped the phone into a voluminous beach bag, and only then did she deign to let her gaze track over to Dax.

He could see the green of her eyes from here. It was like an electric shock straight into his bloodstream. Her smile faded. Dax stood up and walked over, through the bar, and saw her gaze tracking his progress.

He noted that her security team didn't move. Just watched carefully. He realised something then. He leaned against a wooden post beside her table and folded his arms across his chest.

'How long have you known I was here?'

She started to put away her laptop, and a notebook full of scribbles, not looking at him. 'We knew as soon as you boarded the flight in Kuala Lumpur. We've been tracking you since you landed in Langkawi two days ago.'

'Did it amuse you to wait and let me find you?'

She looked up briefly, that vivid green gaze barely skating over him. A not-so-subtle insult. He was used to women looking and lingering. But to this woman he was inconsequential. A novelty.

She said in a clipped voice, 'Not particularly.'

She stood up and Dax realised she was wearing a turquoise blue one-piece swimsuit under cut-off shorts. The floaty vibrantly coloured wrap couldn't disguise her perfect body. Not an inch of excess flesh. She veered towards an athletic physique, but she still had curves in all the right places.

Dax had to force his gaze up from where the swells of her breasts were barely contained by the thin material of the swimsuit. Since when were one-pieces provocative?

Her naturally olive skin was evidence of the same ancestry as Dax. A mixture of Spanish, Italian, Moorish and Greek.

He asked, 'Can I have my phone back, please?'

She looked at him. 'That depends on what you intend to use it for. If it's to divulge my location to your brother, or anyone else, then, no, I'm afraid not.'

Dax was more amused than anything else. There were other means of getting in touch with his brother. 'How do you know I haven't already done that?'

'Because you only knew for certain I was here when you walked into the bar.'

'So you stole my phone?'

She made a *tsk*ing sound. 'I'm not a thief.'

'No, but you employed an innocent child to do your dirty work. What kind of a message is that sending out?'

She flushed at that, and Dax found it inordinately satisfying to see her flustered. How much more satisfying would it be to see her flushed with arousal?

He shifted minutely and cursed his imagination.

Princess Laia said stiffly, 'I told him I knew you and wanted to play a joke on you.'

The fact that she'd considered the integrity of what she was doing sent a dart of something unfamiliar to Dax's gut. A mixture of humour and something soft. *Dangerous*.

He stood up straight. 'Enough chit-chatting, Princess, we both know why I'm here. It's time to come home and fulfil your responsibilities to the people of Santanger.'

Her eyes glittered brightly. 'Santanger is not my home and never will be. I already have a home and responsibilities to my own people.'

Dax studied her, curious about this intransigence. The marriage pact between Santanger and Isla'Rosa made sense on many levels. Not least of which were economic and meant to foster lasting peace in the region. There hadn't been any active wars in at least a couple of generations, but there was still an underlying seam of distrust and enmity between the people in each kingdom, which was having an adverse effect on investment—even in Santanger.

Some investors that Ari and Dax had courted to do business had been put off by the merest hint of potential instability, and it didn't help that things were still stirred up occasionally by very small but effective rebel elements who seemed determined to hang on to the enmity of past generations.

Ari wanted to stamp this out once and for all through his marriage.

But the risk of stirring up unrest was one of the reasons why the marriage agreement between Ari and Laia hadn't been promoted with as much fanfare as would normally be the case. Everyone knew about it, and had known about it for years, but the details—like the wedding date—weren't due to be released until just before the event, to minimise even the small risk of rebellion in either kingdom.

'You know that marrying my brother will bring about a much hoped-for surge in goodwill from both kingdoms that will put an end to any rebel elements for good,' Dax pointed out. 'Not to mention a much-needed injection of capital for development in Isla'Rosa.'

The smaller kingdom was much poorer than Santanger. Santanger had moved with the times and grown into a modern and largely flourishing economy, with a thriving tourist scene for most of the year, thanks to its Mediterranean climate, but Isla'Rosa still lagged far behind.

It was a charming island, and attracted its own loyal tourists, who were captivated by the quaintly medieval capital city and idyllic villages and pristine beaches, but it badly needed hauling into the modern era.

'Your father did your kingdom a disservice by not allowing more growth.'

Princess Laia had gone even pinker now. Dax was momentarily distracted by that wash of blood into her cheeks.

'Don't you dare mention my father. He was a great king and beloved by the people.'

Dax shrugged minutely. 'I'm not disputing that. But our fathers were products of their time—stuck in the past. Santanger has grown and been modernised under my brother, and he can do the same for Isla'Rosa. You know this.'

'I also know that I can do it for Isla'Rosa once I become Queen, and I intend to. On my own.'

She gathered up the bag that held his phone and moved around the table. Dax's gaze tracked down over long, shapely bare legs and pretty feet in sandals.

He realised she was leaving. 'Where are you going?'

'Back to where I'm staying.'

'You have my phone.'

'If you want it you'll have to come with me.'

'I don't intend letting you out of my sight.'

Something flashed across her face at that, but it was gone before Dax could decipher what it was. A curious mixture of fear and something else. But why would she be afraid of him?

She walked out of the bar and Dax saw a slightly battered four-wheel drive appear. The driver—one of the bodyguards—jumped out and held open the back door. Princess Laia got in. Dax went around to the other side and opened the door, to hear Princess Laia say frostily, 'You can ride in the front with Pascal.'

Dax looked at her for a long moment, intrigued by this animosity, and then said, 'As you wish.'

He closed the door and got into the front passenger seat beside the bodyguard, who seemed as frosty as the Princess, not even looking his way.

Another vehicle followed them as they drove away from the beach bar—presumably the second bodyguard. She had good protection at least.

They drove for about fifteen minutes on the main road, with typical Malay houses on either side, built high off the ground to keep them cool in the intense heat. Children scampered about, along with dogs and chickens. A moped overtook them with at least four people on board and a grinning toddler on the lap of the driver. A typical sight in south-east Asia.

Then the vehicles turned down onto a dirt track and they emerged after a couple of minutes into a cleared area, where there was a jetty and two boats bobbing on the water.

They came to a stop. The driver got out and opened the door for Princess Laia. Dax got out too, bemused. A man was on one boat, readying it. Princess Laia walked down the jetty and greeted him in Malay.

Dax noted that the bodyguards carried bags of what looked like groceries and were depositing them in the first boat. Then they got into the other boat, which was

larger—more like a small yacht. He followed them to
the jetty. Princess Laia got into the smaller boat, helped
by the driver.

She turned and looked at Dax. She arched a brow.
'Coming?'

He put his hands on his hips. 'Do I have a choice?'

'Not if you want your phone back.'

'I can get another phone. I know where you are now.'

Princess Laia shrugged. 'Suit yourself. I thought you
were here to take me back, but if you're prepared to risk
me disappearing again...' She trailed off.

Dax gritted his jaw. This magical mystery tour was
beginning to get on his nerves. But he *was* here to bring
her back, so he really couldn't risk watching her sail
off into the sunset and potentially lose her, as she'd just
threatened.

For all he knew she could be on a plane again within
the hour and flitting off to somewhere else.

He stepped into the boat. Princess Laia was sitting
primly on a seat at the back. For all the world like the
Queen she would soon become. Queen of Santanger
and Isla'Rosa. She would be a powerful woman. But
he'd already sensed that power within her.

The driver indicated for Dax to take a seat too, and
he did as he was told. The engines started up and the
boats moved out, the bodyguards staying close.

They hugged the coast of the island for a while before heading out to sea. Just when Dax was beginning
to wonder if they were headed all the way to Thai-
land, an island came into view. Small, and very lush.
As they came closer he could see a pontoon and a beautiful beach.

A wooden structure was just about visible high on a hill, through the thick foliage. It looked like a small palace, with elaborate decorations on the roof reminiscent of royal Thai palaces.

The engine went silent as the driver guided the boat in alongside the fixed pontoon. Dax saw that the bigger boat stayed out on the almost luminously green water.

Princess Laia stood up and lifted some of the bags onto the pontoon. Then she stepped out. He followed her, feeling as bemused as ever.

When he was out, the driver handed him some bags. He saw that they held supplies of vegetables and other food and domestic items.

He heard the engine start again and looked up to see the driver untying the boat. It was soon chugging away from the pontoon. The other boat containing the bodyguards was still some distance away.

He watched the driver wave cheerily at Princess Laia as she said something in Malay. He looked at the Princess, who was regarding him with a suspiciously triumphant glint in her green gaze.

His own narrowed. 'What the hell is this?'

'It's an island called Permata. That's "jewel" in Malay. It belonged to my mother and now it belongs to me.'

He hadn't meant that and she knew it. He'd meant what the hell was this situation. 'Why has the boat left?'

'Because he was only dropping us off.'

'How do we get off this island?'

'We don't. Unless I call for the boat or ask Pascal and Matthew to come and get us. I wouldn't recommend swimming—there are dangerous currents in the waters even though it looks safe.'

It was sinking in. With a slow certainty that was almost embarrassing. She'd caught him out.

Dax put down the bag he was holding and held out a hand. 'My phone, please.' He would arrange transport off this island with her on board within the hour.

Princess Laia held up a finger, as if just remembering. 'Ah…'

She opened her bag and scrabbled around for what seemed like long minutes. Dax's frustration and irritation were growing by the second.

'Dammit, Princess—'

She held up the phone triumphantly, with a smile. 'Got it.'

And, as he watched, she flung it out to the side and it landed in the sea with a loud *splosh*.

Her eyes went wide. 'Oops. Butterfingers.'

She picked up a couple of bags full of shopping and started to walk towards the beach and the lush hill beyond.

Dax just stood there, absorbing what had happened, looking at the place where his phone was undoubtedly sinking to the sea bed.

She stopped and looked back. 'We're the only ones here, so if you want to eat you'll need to bring those bags with you. There are a lot of steps up to the villa— you don't really want to have to make two trips.'

Dax looked at the array of bulging bags at his feet on the pontoon. Then up again. Then out to sea, where the boat that had brought them was disappearing back to the bigger island, not even visible from here.

The other boat was bobbing gently in the sea. Obviously anchored. No sign of the bodyguards. No sign of help.

Dax almost felt like throwing his head back and barking out a laugh. It had been a long time, if ever, since someone had surprised him so effectively. Taken him unawares. Blindsided him. But she'd done it with ruthless and efficient precision.

She'd basically kidnapped him, and all without hitting him over the head or disabling him. He'd followed her every step of the way into this lush and humid paradise.

CHAPTER TWO

PRINCESS LAIA DIDN'T dare look around again to see if he was behind her. Crown Prince Dax de Valle y Montero. One of the most eligible bachelors on the planet. Renowned for his good looks and sybaritic lifestyle. Renowned for lots more. Innuendo and rumours swirled around the man like a mist—not least about his sexual prowess. But she pushed that incendiary thought out of her head.

It was almost a relief to know who had come to find her and have the situation contained. Because she'd known that King Aristedes wouldn't put up with her avoidance of their arranged marriage for much longer. He'd shown his determination to force her to comply by following her to a famously remote festival in the middle of the desert just a few days ago.

Luckily, she'd managed to evade him again. But only just.

The wedding was due to take place in two weeks. Just before her twenty-fifth birthday. As agreed by her father and the previous King of Santanger. A perfectly acceptable agreement on many levels, as Prince Dax had pointed out.

But from the moment she'd been told she would have to marry a crown prince from another kingdom... a complete stranger...when she'd been just ten years old, something inside her had rebelled against it.

And that feeling had only grown stronger over the years, reinforced the few times she'd met King Aristedes—eight years her senior. He'd always seemed aloof and impossibly serious. Not remotely interested in her... in who she really was. She'd felt no connection.

And then, when her father had been dying, four years ago, he'd taken Laia's hand and said, 'My darling, don't marry for anything less than love, no matter how high the stakes. You need to be supported by someone who adores you. This job is hard and long and you deserve to be happy doing it.'

Laia's mother had died giving birth to her, and her father had lived his life in love with a ghost, devoted to her memory. He hadn't ever bowed under the pressure to marry again and have more heirs, telling people, 'I have my heir. Laia will be a great queen one day...'

And that was what the people believed, and what Laia had believed—until he'd revealed a cataclysmic secret. That he'd had a grief-fuelled affair a year after his wife had died.

Even though Laia had had time to absorb that information—and everything else that had come with it— she'd found it hard to let go of the idealised vision of love that her father had presented for so long, in spite of her knowledge of his affair.

Witnessing his devotion to his deceased wife had instilled within Laia a deep yearning for someone to love her in the same way. Yet with that came a sense of guilt—because Laia had killed her mother. Oh, she knew she hadn't *really*, but deep down, in some place where cellular memory was held, she felt guilty. Responsible.

All she had of her mother were inanimate pictures and some video footage of a beautiful, vibrant woman. She'd never been able to look at them without feeling that awful sense of guilt mixed with a hollow feeling of abandonment.

That sense of yearning for a deep and abiding connection had become even more charged as she'd grown up. As if she had a duty and responsibility not to become cynical—even after learning of her father's affair. But to honour her mother's sacrifice, and her father's grief, by aspiring to the ideals they'd set.

And now here she was, hiding out in a tropical paradise avoiding an arranged marriage, because she desperately wanted something *more* than just to be a box ticked on King Aristedes's list of things to do.

Royal wife acquired: *tick*.

Apart from that desire for a great love and supportive companionship instilled within her by her father, she also had an almost primal instinct to protect Isla'Rosa's independence. When her father had signed the marriage agreement all those years ago he'd agreed to make sure the marriage would take place before Laia's birthday, so she would have a husband and King by her side when she was crowned Queen. He'd been worried the pressure of doing it alone would be too much.

But as she'd grown up, and shown her intelligence and strength, he'd confided in her that he thought he'd make a mistake. That he should have ensured she would become Queen first, giving her more power.

Once Laia knew that her father had doubts and regrets it galvanised her to do everything she could to get out of it. She knew Isla'Rosa was badly in need of modernisation and economic assistance—she didn't need a playboy Prince to point that out. But she was determined to do it on her own and find love in the process. On her terms.

She refused to give in to the urge to look behind her to check if Prince Dax was following. Maybe he was still on the pontoon, raging at her for outwitting him.

She could still see the laser-like intensity of his blue eyes. Unusual and distinctive. She'd only seen him up close twice before, because in spite of the marriage agreement most of the meetings had taken place between the Kings, and then between Aristedes and Laia. But even those had been infrequent, due to her reluctance to meet with him.

The most recent occasion had been at a nightclub in Monaco. Unusually for her, in a social situation like that, she'd found herself lingering. For once rebelling at the constraints she'd put on herself.

In a bid to get out of her arranged marriage, she'd perfected the art of seeming to appear at every glittering social gathering she could attend, hoping she would put off the famously serious and conservative King Aristedes from marrying someone who didn't seem remotely inclined to settle down.

Ironically, she had more in common with the King than she did with his feckless playboy younger brother, even if she'd been acting the opposite. But her strategy clearly hadn't worked. Hence her current predicament—sequestering herself on an island with the last man she would choose to spend time with.

So sure about that, Princess? whispered a mischievous little voice.

She tried to block it out, but her memory transported her back to that night in Monaco with humiliating vividness.

That night she'd felt restless. Full of an uncharacteristic sense of missing out on… Fun? Her youth? The music had called to her and she'd found herself on the dance floor, closing her eyes, letting herself believe for a moment that she wasn't Crown Princess Laia Sant Roman, Queen-in-waiting, with a huge responsibility on her shoulders. A responsibility she'd borne all her life as the only heir. She'd wanted to pretend that she was just a regular young woman, with little on her mind but normal worries and concerns.

And then she'd felt an awareness. Like a faint breeze. Raising the tiny hairs on her arms. She'd opened her eyes and a man had filled her vision. Tall and broad. Unmistakably powerful. A very masculine contrast to the far more metrosexual crowd around them. As if he was from another time.

And those eyes… As blue as the clearest sea around Isla'Rosa. Laia had felt an immediate primal pull. As if on some level she'd recognised a mate. She'd wanted to take a step towards him. Absurdly. She'd even gestured to her security team that it was okay to let him approach.

And it had only been then, after her helpless reaction, that she'd realised belatedly who was standing in front of her. Crown Prince Dax. The world's most debauched and spoiled bachelor prince. The spare to the heir.

Immediately she'd felt exposed. And resentful at the brutal reminder that she wasn't just a regular young woman enjoying a carefree night out.

Along with the resentment had come a dart of envy for his freedom, and that had only made her feel even more antagonistic towards him.

To feel envy for that man was shameful.

How could she find him remotely attractive?

He epitomised everything she didn't want in a partner. The only form of love he appeared to know was self-love. He let his brother carry the full weight of responsibility for their royal obligations while he spent his days in dissolute hedonism, travelling from party to party.

As do you.

But she didn't. Not really. And that was all over now anyway. Her plan hadn't worked and now it was just a waiting game until she could return to Isla'Rosa for her birthday and the coronation.

But even if you don't marry this king now you will have to marry soon. And well. What if you never find someone who will love you the way you want? What if King Aristedes is your best chance of a happy life? Even if you don't love each other?

Laia could feel the sweat breaking out on her brow and at the small of her back as she made her way up the steps to the villa through the forest, and it wasn't just due to the high temperatures.

Lately she'd been feeling more and more claustrophobic, as if the walls were encroaching on her. What if she was painting herself into a corner and making a huge mistake, insisting on maintaining her independence and that of her country?

She forced the sensation of claustrophobia out. She reassured herself she was doing the right thing...not selling out her country to let it be subsumed by the bigger and wealthier Santanger. It wasn't the easy option, no doubt about that, but she didn't want the easy option.

She wanted to do things her way, and she wanted a life with someone she could love and respect. Not a marriage based only on duty.

Had it been totally crazy to all but kidnap Prince Dax? *Yes.* But there was no going back now.

For a louche playboy, Prince Dax had managed to find her—which had been no mean feat. So she needed her wits about her. Clearly he was able to focus when he needed to, and she had a sense that she shouldn't underestimate him.

Breathing with a bit of effort when she got to the top of the steps, she turned around—and almost fell backwards when Prince Dax appeared right behind her, taller than she'd expected. He showed no signs of exertion.

She felt churlish. Shouldn't he be a little overweight and soft around the jowls after all his partying? Instead he looked more like a prize athlete.

He stopped and looked around, taking in the open courtyard area in front of the villa with its central pond, where big golden fish swam around lazily. The villa soared dramatically above them, built on three levels. The ground floor was dramatically open to the elements, but there were screens and shutters that protected it during the rainy season.

'This is a rainforest,' Prince Dax said, looking around at the lush vegetation and tall trees.

Laia was tempted to say something snarky, but she settled for, 'Yes, it is.'

She had to admit that no other person on the planet made her feel so...so prickly and antagonistic. He had done from the moment he'd first registered on her consciousness as the younger brother of King Aristedes. She'd been just sixteen years old. That had been their first meeting.

But she couldn't go there now. Not when those blue eyes—far more alert and incisive than she'd expected—swivelled back to her.

For a moment she couldn't breathe.

Laia hated it that he had such an effect on her. She tried to assure herself she was being ridiculous. He was an undeniably gorgeous man and she was merely re-acting as any red-blooded woman would. A bit galling to be as human as the next woman—or man, for that matter—but there was no accounting for hormones. It was also galling that he appeared to be the only man yet to engage her libido.

She was afraid that meeting him again face to face was only confirming something she'd feared since she'd seen him at that club. That he'd had a profound effect on her at a formative time in her life, at that very first meeting, when she'd been just sixteen—almost as if he'd imprinted on her, leaving an invisible marker on her hormones, in her blood, that had ruined her for all other men. Certainly no one she'd met since had come close to having the same effect on her.

Sending up a silent prayer that she was wrong and

that those hormones would calm down, Laia turned and walked into the villa.

She said over her shoulder, 'The kitchen is this way.'

Dax had no choice but to follow his hostess. He was still reeling a little from what had happened. The fact that he was here. And that his phone was somewhere at the bottom of the Straits of Malacca, being nibbled by fish.

All he could do now was accept his current situation, observe his surroundings, and wait for an opportunity to turn the tables on Princess Laia.

He followed her into a generous open-plan kitchen—lots of wood, from the floors to the ceilings. There was a massive island with a black marble countertop, and she'd put the bags on it. She took off the sunhat and her glossy hair hung long and wavy over her shoulders.

She was already taking the groceries out of the bags, basically behaving as if Dax wasn't even there. As inconsequential as a boat boy who'd merely helped her with her shopping.

For someone who prided himself on not having much of an ego, Dax found his irritation levels spiking again. He couldn't recall ever being so…ignored. Certainly not by someone who had gone to some lengths to bring him somewhere and incarcerate him. Albeit somewhere that seemed to be a luxury private island.

He put the shopping bags down. Princess Laia didn't even look up. She was walking over to the fridge now, the delicate material of her wrap revealing more than disguising the tantalising glimpses of her body. Her legs were long and toned. She was a runner.

Dax lifted his gaze and said, as coolly as he could,

'Well, Princess, now that you have me here, what do you intend to do with me?'

He noticed the slightest jolt in her body as she put something into the fridge. A reaction to his voice. So she wasn't as unaffected as she looked. Perhaps he'd misinterpreted that look of fear back on the main island. Maybe it hadn't been fear as much as apprehension at being alone with him.

Because she was as aware of him as he was of her?

Dax's blood pulsed at that thought. And it shouldn't. He had to control himself.

She turned around and came back to the island to pick up more groceries. She said, 'I intend to make sure you don't give away my location before I'm ready to return home.'

'To Santanger…to your fiancé.'

She'd turned to go back to the fridge, avoiding his eye the whole time. 'I am not his fiancée and I have a home of my own. Isla'Rosa.'

'I think a signed marriage agreement between our fathers would attest to my brother and you being affianced.'

He saw the tension in her body—and then she turned around and looked at him. Another electric jolt went through his body. He ignored it.

She said tightly, 'It's not a law.'

'It's not nothing, either. What about the peace agreement? You'd jeopardise the peace between our kingdoms?'

Her eyes sparked. 'Of course not—that's the last thing I want. But from what I know of King Aristedes, he's not so petty that he will undo years of peace-building just because I don't want to marry him. I am confident we can build a lasting and enduring peace without a marriage of convenience.'

'A royal dynastic marriage is a little more than a marriage of convenience.'

Princess Laia came back over to the island and put her hands on it. She really was extraordinarily beautiful.

'I am aware of that. But as your brother has refused to even listen to my side of things I've had to take matters into my own hands.'

Dax frowned. 'Ari is eminently reasonable…much more so than me.'

Princess Laia shrugged minutely. 'Not in this instance. He sees our marriage as a done deal, and when I try to talk to him about it he's not interested.'

'Why don't you just pick up the phone and talk to him about it now?'

She shook her head. 'And let him know my location? No. It's too late for that. There's no discussion to be had. We're not getting married. I will never become Queen of Santanger.'

Dax folded his arms. 'So if you're here…and so intent on not marrying him…then who is the woman purporting to be you in Santanger right now?'

The Princess went pale. Her mouth closed. Lush lips were sealed. Eyes wide. He saw the shadow of guilt in her expression. So she wasn't entirely comfortable with what she was doing. Dax would exploit that chink of vulnerability mercilessly.

He said, 'Ari knows she's not you because he's sent me after you.'

Princess Laia's jaw clenched. 'How did you find out where I was?'

'Thanks to some disreputable people I know in the security industries, I tracked you to Langkawi.'

She said, 'I guess I shouldn't be surprised that you know people on the margins.'

Dax tensed, surprised at the dart of something that felt suspiciously like hurt. He held back the urge to ask her to clarify what she meant, because he already knew and her opinion shouldn't matter.

He'd honed his own disreputable reputation for so long now that he couldn't remember a time when it hadn't been stained with rumours and innuendo. Lots of people had said things to him over the years and it was like water off a duck's back. But not with this woman. He didn't like that revelation. He barely knew her.

He said, 'So, who is the woman pretending to be you?'

With palpable reluctance, Princess Laia said, 'She's my lady-in-waiting. Her name is Maddi.'

Dax absorbed this. 'I only saw a couple of pictures of them returning to Santanger and getting off the plane. She's uncannily like you. Hence the switch, I presume?'

Princess Laia nodded. Suddenly she did look distinctly guilty. Almost green around the gills.

He said, 'Are you sure you have the stomach for this?'

Her eyes flashed, and Dax found himself welcoming that sign of her spirit. Dark luxuriant hair slipped over one shoulder. It reached almost to the top of her breasts.

'I am absolutely fine with this,' she said. She put out a hand 'Why don't you have a look around? Make yourself at home. And please believe me when I say there is no way off this island without triggering an alarm. There is also no access to any communication devices or the internet, so don't bother looking. The bedrooms are on the third level—a guest suite has been made up for you, it's the first one on the right.'

Mercifully, the man left the kitchen and Laia sagged a little. Being in close proximity to him was like being hooked up to an electric charge. It was impossible to relax.

She continued to put the shopping away, including the bags he'd carried, hoping that doing something mundane would make her feel more centred again. But she couldn't stop her mind going back to that seismic moment when she'd first met him. When she'd been sixteen years old.

She'd been attending a charity polo match with her father in Paris, and Prince Dax had been playing for the European team against a team from South America.

Her eye had been drawn to him like a magnet. She hadn't been able to look away. He'd been so unbelievably—ridiculously—gorgeous. Dark messy hair. Stubbled jaw. A face surely carved by the same artists who had created Greek and Roman statues. A body that was lean but muscled in a way that had made her feel funny inside…as if she'd known that it was something she didn't fully understand yet.

At sixteen she'd been worldly-wise in so many ways, but not when it came to boys—or men.

She'd seen him from a distance before that, once, on a rare trip to the palace in Santanger with her father when she'd been much younger. He'd been a gangly teenager. But in Paris he'd been a man.

The VIP hospitality tent had been alive with whispers and gossip about him. His legendary sexual prowess. His string of lovers. His absolute contempt for showing an atom of responsibility. His poor brother who had to do all the work. And, worse and most salacious of all, the fiercely whispered rumour that he'd been responsible for his mother's tragic and untimely death in a car crash because he'd been driving the car.

That was a scandal in itself, because he'd only been fifteen years old—too young to drive legally. But the Queen's death had been ruled a tragic accident and no further legal proceedings had issued from it. People had commented on the entitlement of the rich and powerful, who felt they were above the law.

So, to say he'd had a reputation as an *enfant terrible* would have been an understatement. He'd appeared after the match in the tent, still wearing his mud-splattered clothes, his dark skin gleaming with perspiration. Obviously uncaring what anyone thought.

Laia would never forget his scent: earth and musky sweat and pure undiluted *male*. As potent as if he'd just climbed out of a lover's bed. She'd been struck mute by his sheer raw magnetism and total insouciance.

He'd seen her father and had come over, and she had been able to tell that her father disapproved of him. They'd greeted one another, though, civilly. And Prince Dax had looked at her then, with an appraising gaze. Laia had been mortified by the flash of heat that had washed through her entire body, making her aware of it in a way she'd never experienced before. Making her aware of the dress she was wearing, which had suddenly felt too tight and childish.

That look alone, along with her awareness of him, had unlocked something inside her. An understanding of herself becoming a woman. A sexual being.

Then he'd said, with casual devastation, 'I believe that one day I'll be your brother-in-law.'

It had taken a moment for his words to sink in. She'd been avoiding thinking about her arranged marriage very well up to that point. But with those few words it had rushed home with the speed of a freight train crashing into her.

The fact that *this man* in front of her, who was causing such a conflicting mix of emotions and sensations in her body and head, was someday going to be sitting at a table, maybe across from her, or beside her, as her *brother-in-law*, had been suddenly horrifying.

So much so that she'd felt sick.

Her father must have seen her reaction, because he'd said something and ushered her away.

He'd put her reaction down to Prince Dax presenting himself in less than pristine condition. But the truth was that for long weeks afterwards Laia had been obsessed with Prince Dax. Looking him up online. Watching his exploits unfold as he made his way from Paris to London, New York to Rome—you name it, he was there— with the world's most beautiful women on his arm and that devil-may-care grin on his face.

Gradually, mortified by her obsession, Laia had convinced herself that he disgusted her. That he revolted her with his blatant lack of consideration for anything but the good life. The incredibly louche life. Serving only himself and—by all accounts—his insatiable appetites. Whether it was for women or experiences or luxury properties or yachts…

But now that he was here, on her beloved island, sequestered with her for at least the next ten days, Laia knew she would have no choice but to face up to the fact that Prince Dax bothered her a lot.

And she was afraid that it was for far more complicated reasons than the simplistic antipathy she'd honed for years. She wasn't normally a judgemental person— never had been. She prided herself on accepting everyone as she met them. Prince Dax, however, had always uniquely got under her skin.

She was afraid that her judgement of the man was about to blow up in her face in spectacular fashion… because really, all along, it had been based on the way he made her feel and not on his lifestyle choices.

Dax stood on the generous outdoor balcony of the guest suite. He had a view out over the treetops to the sea beyond, where he could see the security team's yacht bobbing peacefully on the water. He idly wondered how long it would take to swim to the boat, climb on board, disable the bodyguards and call for help.

But, as appealing as that might be—if a little unrealistic—surely it was more prudent to win the Princess over to accepting her fate rather than coercing her into it. It was the twenty-first century after all. She was clearly a modern woman who was resistant to being treated like a chattel. Not exactly an unreasonable state of affairs.

In many respects, Dax had never really understood

his brother Ari's dogged acceptance of a wedding agreement made when he'd been only eight years old. Princess Laia had been just a baby!

In every other respect his brother was a forward-thinking, modern monarch. But not in this. Even when Dax had brought it up over the years, teasing Ari about what his wife might be like, how he could possibly agree to live with a woman he didn't know, Ari had closed down the discussion. Usually by saying something like, 'You saw how it was between our parents. Do you think I want to risk that again? I'm quite happy to marry for duty and responsibility and siring heirs. I don't want anything more. Princess Laia has been bred for this. She knows the score.'

As if Dax needed any reminder of the hellscape that had been his parents' unhappy marriage… His mother had had the audacity to fall in love with her husband, and the King had repaid her love by taking numerous lovers throughout their union.

It had turned Dax's mother into a brittle and self-destructive shell of a woman. Dax had become her crutch and her confidant well before he should have even known about such things. But with Ari busy with lessons to prepare him for one day becoming sovereign, Dax had been the only one his mother had been able to turn to.

He diverted his mind from toxic memories now. He hadn't thought about such things in a long time, and he didn't welcome their resurgence.

Privately Dax had always thought to himself that while Ari was happy to accept his fate, maybe his future wife would be less so. And that was exactly what had come to pass.

Although he took no pleasure in that. Not when he was captive on a tropical island thousands of miles from his brother in Santanger. Thousands of miles from his own life.

He looked down to the ground level, where a wide lap pool looked very inviting. Sunbeds were laid out around it. The water shimmered green and blue from the mosaics underneath.

He turned around. The bedroom was palatial. Lots of wood, as was the custom in this part of the world. A massive bed dressed in cool white linen. It was a four-poster, with a simple wooden frame from which hung the very necessary mosquito net to protect him from small biting insects at night.

The bathroom was also huge, with a shower that was open to the elements. Very romantic. Dax smiled mirthlessly at the that notion. He was here with a woman who openly disdained him.

He wasn't so arrogant as to think that every woman he met fancied him, but he knew that being blessed with a pleasing physical appearance together with vast personal wealth, both inherited and created, was a powerful cocktail.

For the first time he was in the presence of someone who appeared less than impressed.

Dax spotted another door and opened it. It led into a dressing room. It was full of clothes. All brand-new. With the tags still on. More or less in his size. There was underwear. Swimwear. Leisure wear. Casual clothes. Shoes. There was even a tuxedo.

Dax left his suite to make his way back down to the kitchen, but in the corridor he spotted a door opposite. Her room? Curious, he went and tested the door. It was locked, so presumably it was hers. He had to hand it to her, she was certainly prepared.

He went downstairs to where the Princess was now chopping a range of colourful vegetables. She'd tied her hair back and up into a loose knot, and it exposed the delicate line of her jaw and neck. Her hands were deft. Short, practical nails.

Something moved through Dax at that moment—a fleeting sense of almost...protectiveness.

Rejection of that notion made his voice sharp. 'The dressing room is stocked with clothes. Did kidnapping me interrupt a lover coming to stay?'

She made a face. 'No. And don't you think you're being a little dramatic? Kidnap?'

'What would you call it, then, if not kidnapping?'

She stopped chopping, as if considering this, and then said, 'A momentary redirection.' She added, 'I took the liberty of stocking clothes because I knew you would need them.'

Dax wasn't sure whether to feel amused, bemused or insulted. Or irritated. Very few people had the where-withal to derail his life like this. He didn't like the sensation of being powerless.

'You got the sizes mostly right, but I'm not sure a black tuxedo is entirely necessary.'

She shrugged. 'You know as well as I do that we have to be prepared at all times for any eventuality.'

Dax could appreciate that. As a royal, he did have to

be prepared for literally everything, but somehow he couldn't see a black-tie event in his near future.

Then Dax thought of something—very belatedly. 'I have a hotel room. My things…my passport.'

'Taken care of,' the Princess said briskly. 'I've instructed the hotel to pack your things and put them in the safe until you return to pick them up.'

The irritation spiked. He was a busy man. 'And that would be…when, exactly?'

She looked at him. 'Ten days at the most.'

Enough was enough. 'Look, Princess Laia—'

She put up a hand. 'Please, call me Laia. I don't think we need to stand on formalities here, do we?'

Dax clenched his jaw and then said sweetly, 'Well, seeing as how we're going to be in-laws, no, I guess not. The same goes for you…just Dax will suffice.'

She flushed at that and went back to her chopping. 'I'm making a chicken and vegetable stir-fry for dinner. You're welcome to have some.'

He noted she wasn't inviting him to join her. 'Not exactly what I would have expected a princess to be doing.'

She looked at him. 'Don't judge us all by your standards.'

Dax's gaze narrowed on Laia. He didn't like the way her judgement of him pricked his skin like a sharp knife.

He put his hands on the island. 'You really don't like me, do you? Which is strange, because we don't even know each other. Maybe if you gave me a chance you'd realise that I'm not the person you clearly think I am.'

She went pinker. The fact that she couldn't hide her reactions was fascinating to Dax.

She said, 'Perhaps. But we're not really here to get acquainted.'

Dax's blood grew warm at the thought of getting 'acquainted'. He resisted her statement. It made him feel rebellious. Like forgetting he had a duty to his brother where this woman was concerned.

He wanted her.

And he'd wanted her since he'd seen her in that club. He had a feeling it was going to get harder to ignore.

'Well, maybe you should have thought about that before sequestering us on a private island with—as far as I can make out—not a whole lot to do.'

She visibly gulped at that, but it was little comfort. The magnitude of what had happened seemed to hit Dax at that moment, and suddenly he felt as caged as a captive tiger, even within this lush paradise.

With exaggerated care he said, 'Thank you for the offer of food, but I'll look after myself. I would have contributed to the shopping if I'd known what to expect.'

Laia's eyes darted to him as if she was sensing his sudden volatility. 'That's okay… We have enough supplies. There'll be leftovers if you change your mind.'

Dax turned and walked away, exerting every atom of control he could muster. He had operated outside of his comfort zone for a long time, so this situation was irritating but not disconcerting. But what he wasn't prepared for was the feeling of emotional exposure. And no way was he going to let Laia see how she affected him.

CHAPTER THREE

LAIA QUESTIONED HER sanity in thinking this was a viable
option. She'd sensed Dax's volatility just now—like a
crackling forcefield around him. She could only wonder
how she would feel if she was in his shoes. A lot more
vulnerable, for a start. Angry. *Helpless.*

Her conscience pricked hard.

Although the last thing he struck her as was helpless. In fact she wouldn't put it past him to swim out
to the security boat, overcome the guards and take off.
He seemed entirely capable.

But if he tried that he would set off the alarm and
they'd be ready for him.

In fact, when she thought about it, he wasn't behaving as she might have expected of a playboy who was
used to instant gratification and the constant stimula-
tion of beautiful women and places. He didn't seem to
be hugely perturbed. Annoyed, yes, but not petulant
that he was missing whatever nightclub opening he was
due to attend.

Laia scowled at herself. It wasn't like her to be bitchy.
But this man appealed to her worst qualities.

*Because he affects you, and you're not honest enough
to acknowledge how much.*

She scowled even more.

She diverted her brain away from such uncomfortable things by focusing on what she *should* be thinking about. Or *who*. Maddi, her lady-in-waiting and best friend. And, more sensationally, her half-sister, who was the product of the affair her father had had with a woman from the castle staff.

No one but them knew that they were sisters.

Her father had told her he'd always regretted how he'd handled it, because when he'd found out his lover was pregnant he'd sent her away, for fear of a scandal. He'd asked Laia to go and find her sister and tell her he was sorry.

Apparently Maddi, who lived in Ireland, had always known who she was and where she came from.

After her father's death, Laia had been too grief-struck and shocked to go looking for her half-sister. And then, as time had passed, she'd grown apprehensive. Afraid of what she might find.

Someone who was resentful? Angry? Vengeful?

But eventually Laia had been able to ignore her conscience no longer and she'd gone to Ireland. And when she had found her half-sister Maddi had been none of the things Laia had feared.

Maddi had been shy. And yet there had been a strong bond between them from the moment they'd met. Laia had begged her sister to come to Isla'Rosa with her, to see where she came from. Maddi was the one who'd suggested working as Laia's lady-in-waiting, to give her a chance to be anonymous and learn more about

Laia and everything. They'd agreed that Laia's coronation would be the opportune time to reveal Maddi as a member of the royal family.

Over the past year they'd forged an even stronger bond and had become inseparable. So when King Aristedes had followed them to that festival in the desert just days ago, demonstrating his determination to make Laia his wife, Maddi had suggested taking advantage of the fact that they were so alike they could pass for twins.

Before Laia had known what was happening she'd been bundled away by her security team and Maddi had taken off in a small sleek jet with King Aristedes, pretending to be her.

But obviously, since Dax had been on her trail so soon after their switch, Maddi's impersonation of Laia couldn't have lasted more than a few hours after her arrival with the King into Santanger.

Maddi had sent her a text—obviously before she'd known the King had discovered their ruse—saying that the King believed she was Laia, that she was okay, and asking where Laia was. Laia had responded—but only mentioning that she was in south-east Asia, for fear of someone taking Maddi's phone. Since then there had been no more messages.

She knew Maddi was capable of looking after herself—she was a lot more street smart than Laia, thanks to having lived a regular life. And King Aristedes was a civilised man. He wouldn't want adverse press at this time any more than she did, which was presumably why he wasn't exposing his fake fiancée.

He would undoubtedly be expecting his brother to

reappear at any moment, with Laia by his side. Was he hoping to merely switch his fake fiancée for his real one? Well, that wasn't going to happen. Once.

Laia was Queen she would be in a much stronger position to negotiate with King Aristedes—about their marriage *and* peace.

All she had to do was bide her time here until a couple of days before her birthday.

Here, on a romantic private island, with the one man in the world who makes you feel prickly and hot and full of a need you can't even name.

Laia pushed that incendiary thought out of her head and focused on cooking the food. She wasn't remotely Dax's type—not that she wanted to be, she assured herself hurriedly.

For one thing, he always seemed to favour tall, slim blondes. A dramatic contrast to his dark good looks. And she was far too boring and staid for his tastes.

The persona she'd created of being a party girl was paper-thin. She'd become an expert at appearing at the opening of an event only to be curled up in bed with a book an hour later, with no one any the wiser. She'd realised that once people *saw* you there, they just assumed you were there for the night. And she'd always made sure she appeared in the press.

Within a couple of days her guest would be climbing the trees with boredom, but there was nothing Laia could do to help that. There was no way she was jeopardising her future when she was close enough to feel the weight of the Isla'Rosa crown on her head and know that she was taking her own destiny, and that of her country, into her own hands and no one else's.

* * *

Later that evening Dax wandered into the kitchen, rubbing his wet hair with a towel. He'd just had a shower in the changing gazebo after a swim in the lap pool, and felt marginally less edgy and irritated after expending some energy.

He'd walked around the island a little beforehand. It was mostly forest and precipitous hills. There was a stunning private white sand beach on the other side of the island. And a small house that he guessed was used by staff when they were required.

It was indeed a beautiful location. But Laia was right. Unless he dived into the sea and started swimming he wasn't going anywhere.

And now, after the activity, he was hungry. He opened the fridge and spotted a Tupperware bowl filled with the leftovers of the stir-fry. There was a Post-it note attached.

Feel free to help yourself.

Strange to feel somewhat mollified at this very basic concession for having removed him from his life so spectacularly. But then hadn't he been planning on doing that to Laia? Albeit without resorting to kidnap. He could see now, though, that she wouldn't have gone anywhere with him willingly.

He took out the bowl and lifted off the airtight lid. It smelled good. His stomach rumbled. Dax had always had a healthy appetite. For everything. Life. Sex. Ambition. Winning. *Sex.*

He hadn't had sex for a few months. It had been preying on his mind…the flatlining of his libido. But lately everything had begun to feel a little dull. There was no excitement. No one causing his pulse to trip.

Until he'd laid eyes on Laia again today.

He set about putting the stir-fry in the microwave, and tried not to think about the suspicion that he'd actually felt flat since he'd seen her in that nightclub over a year ago.

Oh, he'd taken lovers since then. But for the first time it hadn't been satisfying. And so he'd subconsciously taken a hiatus from women. Focused instead on his work.

He'd even taken a call from Ari a month or so ago, his brother commenting, 'You haven't appeared in the papers in a few weeks. I'm just checking you're still alive.'

Dax had realised with a jolt that he hadn't had any appetite for going out. For the endless round of socialising that for so long had helped him not to think about things.

He'd replied, 'I'm very much alive, brother. Maybe I'm plotting to take over your throne? It's all the rage on every TV show at the moment.'

Ari had sounded weary. 'Be my guest—and while you're at it see if you can track down Princess Laia and remind her of her marital obligations, would you?'

Dax had responded lightly, belying the spike of something sharp in his gut that had felt suspiciously like jealousy. 'Maybe she's just not that into you.'

His brother had said, 'Ha-ha,' and terminated the call.

And now he was here, with this woman who appealed to him in a way that was seriously unwelcome, and instead of being able to explore his attraction as he usually would—by seduction and indulging in slaking his desires—he had to do the right thing and encourage her go back to Europe, marry his brother and become his sister-in-law. His Queen.

Once again the resistance he felt to that idea was almost physical.

The microwave dinged at that moment and Dax welcomed the distraction. He took out the bowl of stir-fry and transferred it to a plate. He got himself a beer from the fridge, and went to sit on the decking outside the kitchen.

Dusk was cloaking everything in a lush lavender colour. The night chorus of insects was starting up. Dax noticed a citronella candle burning, to deter mosquitoes. Had Laia been sitting here eating just a short while before?

The food was delicious. Fresh and tasty, with a bit of a kick. Dax wolfed it down.

Laia was an enigma, for sure—a queen in waiting so desperate not to be married that she had run to the other side of the world to a jungle paradise where she seemed happy to cook and wait on herself.

Not the behaviour he would have expected of someone of her standing. He knew people with regular blood running through their veins who wouldn't deign to lower themselves to such mundane activities.

He was going to do his utmost to figure out how to get to her and make her see sense, and then he'd send her on her way before she could wrap his brain—*and his body*—into too many knots.

The following morning, after a fractious sleep that she blamed Dax for, Laia felt fuzzy-headed even after a swim in the pool and a shower. She went down to the kitchen, taking out supplies for breakfast. Pastries and fruit and granola. She made coffee and the fragrant smell helped clear her head.

She had to admit moodily that her sleep had also been fractious because she was sharing a space with a man who made her feel aware of herself as a woman, and very conscious of the fact that she was that rare unicorn: a virgin. Still. At almost twenty-five.

In her defence, she wasn't exactly in a position where she could indulge in carnal activities without risking drawing the all-seeing eye of the press. If anything, seeing Dax's sexploits splashed routinely across the tabloids over the years had put the fear of God into her. And as time had gone on, and she'd grown older, the world's fascination with her and her love-life had assumed gargantuan proportions, making it even more unlikely that she would indulge.

Not that she'd met anyone who'd made her feel like indulging.

Except for the man who is here right now, in your house...

She pushed that inflammatory thought aside. And then she heard a sound and looked up and froze, even while simultaneously melting on the spot.

Dax was on the other side of the kitchen, having just walked in from outside.

He was bare-chested and wearing a pair of short sweatpants. He was drinking from a bottle of water. Laia was aware that he must have been running, or maybe he'd found the gym.

Her gaze seemed to be glued to his chest. It wasn't

the first time she'd seen a bare-chested man, but it felt like it.

He was...sublime. Broad and exquisitely muscled. A light smattering of hair across his pectorals met in a line that dissected his abdominal muscles and continued down under the top of his shorts...

Laia raised her eyes, cheeks on fire. Dammit, why couldn't she be cool? She'd never needed to be cool more than now. She felt ridiculously overdressed, in a loose linen sleeveless shirt and loose trousers. Then she noticed something else. A dark mark high over one pectoral.

He walked closer. She could see that it was a tattoo.

'You have a tattoo.'

She wasn't sure why she was surprised. It wasn't as if this man didn't have a reputation for being a rebel already.

The ink drawing was surprisingly delicate and beautiful. An intricate birdcage with a closed door and a bird inside. For some reason it made Laia feel a little sad.

'The bird is caged.'

She looked at Dax and saw he was watching her with a wary expression. It diffused something inside her... as if she'd discovered a chink in his armour.

'Yes, the bird is caged.'

'Does it mean something?'

An expression crossed his face so fleetingly that she might have imagined it, but she knew she hadn't. It had been *pain*.

He shrugged minutely. 'It was done on a drunken whim. It means whatever you want it to mean.'

'Drunken tattoos aren't usually as...considered.'

He arched a brow. 'Maybe you'd like to tell me what you think it means?'

The air around them seemed to have grown thick and charged. Laia was glad of the big solid island between them.

She changed the subject. 'Did you go for a run?' she babbled. 'We have a gym, too, fully equipped.'

'I found the gym, thank you.'

She put some fruit and yoghurt into a bowl and said, 'Please, help yourself to whatever you'd like. There's fresh coffee.'

She moved to a table on the terrace before Dax could get too close as he filled his own plate with a little of everything. He was a big man—he undoubtedly had a healthy appetite.

Not just for food, whispered a little wicked voice.

Laia tensed all over as Dax came over and joined her at the table.

He stopped before sitting down. 'Do you mind?'

Yes. She shook her head. 'Of course not.'

He sat down. Laia felt uptight. His chest filled her peripheral vision. She wanted to ask him to put a top on, but they were in the tropics. It was entirely practical to wear as little as possible. His skin gleamed. From the humidity or from exertion? She had an urge to go closer, to breathe in his scent.

This awareness of herself as a woman and him as a very masculine man made her skin prickle uncomfortably. She cursed silently. Why couldn't she be immune to him?

'So, this island…it belongs to you?' he asked.

Laia nodded, glad of a diversion from her increasingly heated thoughts. 'It was my mother's—left to her by an uncle who lived here his whole life.'

'Your mother, Queen Isabel, had links to almost every royal family in Europe.'

Laia looked at Dax. He sat in a louche sprawl on the other side of the table. Supremely at ease. Not ranting and raving about being incarcerated. She didn't trust it for a minute.

She took a sip of coffee and nodded. 'As do we all.'

'True.'

In fact he was being polite. Civil. Laia could play him at his own game and be polite too. 'Have you been to Malaysia before?'

Dax nodded his head. 'Yes, but only to Kuala Lumpur. I am grateful for an opportunity to explore more of this beautiful country.'

Laia looked at Dax suspiciously. He had an innocent expression, as if to say, *What?* She felt a little disconcerted. She wasn't sure how to handle this sanguine man who appeared to hold no grudge for her having removed him from his life for an extended period.

Her conscience forced her to say, 'Look, I'm sorry that it had to happen like this. I'm sure you're missing lots of…engagements. I hope nothing too important?'

Dax took a sip of coffee and put the cup down. He said, 'I'd already carved time out of my schedule because my brother asked me to track you down. And that's what I've done. But I won't consider the job done until you are delivered to him in Santanger.'

Laia scowled. 'Like a parcel.'

Dax shook his head. 'Like the wife you agreed to be.'

Now Laia shook her head. 'I never agreed to it. I was

never given a chance. It was a *fait accompli* from the day I was born and born a girl. How archaic is that?'

His eyes narrowed on her. 'It's the way it's done in our world. You do know that there are far more arranged marriages than so-called love matches globally?'

'You're not a fan of a love match, then?'

Now he was the one who looked slightly uncomfortable, avoiding her eye. Laia felt it like a small triumph.

He said, 'Not for people like us, no.'

'But normal people can indulge?'

He looked at her. 'The stakes are lower.'

That was one way of putting it. The stakes were definitely lower when you didn't have a duty to a nation of people and the responsibility of continuing a royal line.

Laia felt a dart of guilt before she realised that this was probably Dax's plan—to undermine her resolve.

As if reading her mind, he asked congenially, 'Why are you so against the marriage? Ari isn't a bad person. I'm told he's considered to be quite attractive.' Dax made a self-deprecating face. 'Not as much as me, of course, but he can't have everything—the kingdom *and* incredible sex appeal.'

Laia had to curb the urge to roll her eyes and smile at his confidence.

He's a charmer, reminded a little voice. *This is how he's spent his dissolute life. This is how he's trying to get to you, any way possible.*

Laia sobered. 'I'm not against marriage. I'm just against this one. Your brother has no interest in me. He expects a convenient royal wife to slot into his world and doesn't want to discuss it further.'

'So what is it that you want, if not a perfectly reasonable match with one of the world's wealthiest and most eligible men? Call me old-fashioned, but I can't see many women turning that opportunity down.'

'You're cynical.'

He looked surprised. 'And you're not?'

Laia shook her head. How had they got into this territory? 'I try not to be. I want a deeper partnership with my husband.'

A smile spread across Dax's face and Laia's breath got stuck in her throat for a second. When he smiled it was like being caught in the sun's rays...magnetic and—

He declared, 'You're a romantic.'

Laia went cold. Was she so transparent? She felt exposed under Dax's gaze.

'Don't be ridiculous.'

He shrugged. 'If you gave Ari a chance you might find that your relationship provides all that you need.'

'I did try to talk to him—after my father's funeral. He wasn't interested. He said the marriage would be happening and there was nothing further to discuss. He had his chance to convince me and now it's gone.'

Suddenly Dax looked serious. 'It's a fool's errand, looking for love in our world. It simply doesn't exist—and nor would you want it to. It only leads to self-destruction.'

Laia frowned. 'What does that mean? Who are you talking about?'

But Dax had stood up abruptly. He said, 'I'm going to clean up. Can I ask you to pass a message to one of my assistants for me? I'm sure you don't want worldwide headlines shouting about the missing Playboy Prince.'

Laia took the abrupt hint. Clearly he didn't like her question and wasn't going to answer.

She considered his request and knew she owed him this much. 'Okay.' She stood up and went to a drawer, pulling out a notepad and a pen. She handed it to Dax. 'Give me the details.'

But he said, 'I'll call them out to you, if you don't mind. I'm dyslexic, so it'll take me longer to write it all down.'

Laia stopped and looked at him. She hadn't expected him to say that. And so easily.

'I...' For once in her life she felt at a loss. Not sure what to say. Eventually she said, 'I'm sorry. I wasn't expecting to hear you say that. I didn't know you were dyslexic.'

Dax looked unperturbed. 'Both me and my brother have it—him to a lesser degree. I've learnt to navigate my way around it.'

Laia felt as if the ground was shifting under her feet. This threw a new perspective on Dax. An intriguing one.

'Okay, call out the details.'

He did, and she wrote them down. When she looked up again Dax was too close. That chest was all she could see. And she could smell his scent. Woodsy and musky. She had the most bizarre urge to put her hand on his chest and feel his heart beating against her palm.

She backed away so fast she almost fell over.

She said, 'I'll do this now,' and fled.

Dax could still smell Laia's scent lingering in the air. Soft and flowery. But not too sweet. There was something sharp. Like her.

She'd looked at him sharply just now, when he'd told her he had dyslexia. As if reassessing him. He was used to people looking at him differently when they found out—and not necessarily kindly. Sometimes with pity. Sometimes as if his diagnosis explained something to them. As if it explained why he was nothing but a feckless royal playboy—because how could anyone with dyslexia be successful?

A total misconception, as Dax knew well. Some of the most successful people in the world had dyslexia and similar neurodivergences.

But he had been a feckless royal playboy in his younger years. So he couldn't really blame people for their lazy judgement. And if they continued to judge him based on that earlier version of himself then more fool them. And he'd proved lots of people to be fools by now.

He realised that he'd mentioned his dyslexia just now because he'd wanted to see how Laia would respond. He'd almost wanted to see that glint of *aha* in her eyes, as if she could square him away into a little box. Dismiss him.

But she hadn't looked at him like that. She'd been surprised, but not judgemental. Intrigued. She was endlessly surprising. Not least for pulling this stunt in getting him onto a private island with no escape.

And also because sometimes she looked at him the way she had in Monte Carlo, with big eyes. As if she'd never seen a man before.

As if she wanted to devour him.

But in the next second the shutters would come

down and she'd disappear back behind an expression-
less mask, like she had that night.

She reminded him of a fawn. Curious, but drawing back.

She wanted him. He knew that now.

Her little glances when she thought he wasn't looking.

The way she quivered when he came near.

The almost ever-present flush in her cheeks—
although admittedly sometimes that might be irritation or anger.

And you want her.

Dax turned and strode out to the terrace, to try and
cool the heat in his body and brain. He might want her,
but he couldn't have her. Not this woman who'd been
promised to his brother from her birth.

He cursed. It *was* archaic. It was ridiculous. But it
was her destiny and he had to do everything in his
power to make sure it happened.

His brother had let him have his freedom and now
it was Dax's turn to give Ari what he needed. A wife
and a queen.

A little later, Laia was sitting cross-legged on her bed
with her bedroom door carefully locked. She was on
her laptop, which was hooked up to rapid broadband.

There were no headlines mentioning anything about
Dax going missing. There were, however, some headlines about Princess Laia's arrival on Santanger, and
speculation about the royal wedding but no real details.

King Aristedes must have realised that he'd have to
postpone the wedding at the very least.

There were several grainy pictures of Maddi arriving in Santanger, wearing what looked like a man's jacket and with long bare legs. And then there were more recent pictures of her and the King at a palace garden party.

Laia touched the screen. Maddi looked very sleekly polished and a little terrified beside the tall and stern King. Wide-eyed. Obviously the King *was* determined to maintain the fiction of his wedding proceeding, and luckily no one had seemed to notice that Maddi wasn't Laia.

They looked so alike. It was only at close quarters that someone might notice that Maddi's eyes were darker and that she was a little curvier—much to Laia's envy.

The fact that the King hadn't noticed that Maddi wasn't Laia from the very first moment told Laia she was doing the right thing. They might not have spent much time together but he knew her well enough to have noticed. If he cared.

Laia hoped that Maddi was coping okay, and vowed to get her back to Isla'Rosa just as soon as she could. Her heart swelled as she thought of what her sister had done for her so selflessly.

Laia had spoken to her most trusted and closest advisor, who supported everything she was doing. He was the only one outside of Maddi, King Aristedes and Dax who knew exactly what was going on and where she was.

She'd just had a video meeting with him, to make sure all was proceeding as planned and that nobody suspected anything was awry. The Privy Council—

the group of traditionalist men who'd worked for her father and who Laia had every intention of disbanding once she became Queen, to make way for a much more gender-equal and inclusive council—were under the impression that she was, indeed, in Santanger, fulfilling her engagement duties. Thanks to Maddi.

They wouldn't know any different until she came back to Isla'Rosa, just before the coronation was due to take place. There would be repercussions from breaking the engagement, but nothing she couldn't handle.

So now she turned to the piece of paper where she'd written down *Montero Holdings* along with Dax's assistant's email address. The name Montero Holdings rang a small bell, but she couldn't place where she'd heard it before.

Laia sent his assistant an email from a generic account, explaining that she was acting on Dax's behalf for a few days, and giving a set of instructions regarding launching a new software product online in the coming weeks. And another instruction regarding sending his apologies for not being able to make the board meeting of a charity that—

Laia stopped typing and sat back. She hadn't fully taken in what she was writing down at the time. The New Beginnings charity was very close to Laia's own heart. She'd donated generously over the years—usually anonymously.

It had been set up specifically to target babies, children and minors who had been left orphaned or alone after either a natural disaster or through migration, when they were most vulnerable and prey to being trafficked or exploited. The charity provided safe places to stay, education and resources to help them find permanent homes. It also provided scholarships for sports academies and third level education.

It was an amazing charity, and it had called to Laia as soon as she'd heard about it. Her circumstances had been vastly different, of course—she'd still had a loving father—but she'd always felt the loss of her mother so keenly, and could empathise with other children bearing that huge loss.

As far as she could make out Dax was on the board of this charity. *Interesting...* A lot of wealthy people paid lip service to charities—she'd seen photographic evidence of Dax attending enough events over the years, with a beautiful woman in tow, and she'd thought it started and ended there.

But being on a board was a responsibility—she knew because she was on a few. You wouldn't be tolerated for long if you didn't pull your weight.

Intrigued, Laia finished sending the email and resisted the urge to dive deeper into an investigation of Dax online.

She thought of the fact that he was dyslexic. The people she knew with dyslexia had had to overcome hurdles most people never had to face. They were incredibly high achievers and very successful. Ingenious.

Laia had to concede that maybe Dax had more substance to him than she'd initially given him credit for, but a man with a social life as busy as his—

A headline popped up on her web browser at that moment and she stopped and clicked on it.

Is Playboy Prince Dax finally settling down?

Below was an article speculating as to what he was

up to, and with whom, because he hadn't been seen on the social circuit in a few months.

The article was from a month or so ago, so it had nothing to do with his current disappearance.

Laia breathed a sigh of relief and absorbed the fact that perhaps Dax didn't seem too put out by his current situation because he'd already been taking time out? For what? *Was* there someone special? Hardly, if he wasn't asking her to let anyone else know he was okay.

For a moment Laia wondered what it would be like to have someone like Dax care enough about you to let you know he was okay. To care enough about him to be worried about him.

She felt a swooping sensation in her lower belly and quickly shut her laptop.

Maybe she would follow Dax's lead and go to the gym…try to work off some of the restless energy she was feeling. She told herself it *wasn't* because she was more acutely aware than ever that she had one of the world's most notorious playboys on her private island and completely at her behest.

The words that he'd said to her on that first day came back in her head. *'Now you have me here, what are you going to do with me?'*

Laia let out a sound of frustration and left her room— but not until she'd made sure it was locked again.

Late that afternoon, Dax was flicking through the apps on the TV in the media room when he heard a sound and looked up to see Laia in the doorway. He went very still.

Every inch of her athletic physique was lovingly outlined by the clinging Lycra of her leggings and the tank top she wore. Her hair was pulled back and up into a ponytail. Her face was clean of make-up. A little shiny from exertion.

Dax's entire body pulsed with awareness and something much more basic—lust.

He realised she was holding something. A mobile phone. She came into the room and said, 'I have your assistant John on the phone. He wants to verify that it is you who is sending the instructions via email.'

Dax stood up. He held out his hand for the phone. But she shook her head.

She said, 'I have it on mute at the moment. I'll put him on speaker.'

Dax almost smiled. It would be nothing for him to take the phone from Laia, but he had to admit that he felt disinclined to do it. He told himself that it was because he knew gaining her trust would be far more effective.

'Okay.' He folded his arms.

Laia unmuted the phone and pressed the speaker button. She said, 'Okay, John, go ahead.'

'Dax, are you there?'

Dax didn't take his gaze off Laia's. 'I'm here. Did you get the email?'

'Yeah… I just wanted to make sure it really was you. What's going on Dax? Is everything okay?'

Laia's finger hovered over the disconnect button.

Dax said, 'Everything is fine. If I need anything else I'll contact you. I'm on a holiday and I don't want to be disturbed unless it's urgent, okay? If my brother calls looking for me, tell him I'm still working on his project.'

His assistant sounded bemused. 'Okay... Dax, do you know how long you'll be on this holiday?'

Laia took the phone off speaker and turned around, saying into it, 'Sorry, John, Dax has just stepped out. He'll be away for at least ten days, okay? Thank you.'

She terminated the call.

But Dax had barely even heard what she'd said because his gaze was glued to her behind. High and firm. More lush than he would have imagined. *Sexy.* He had a sense that she wasn't even aware of that. There was an innocence about her that made him wonder fleetingly if she might still be a virgin. There'd certainly never been any hint of a relationship or even an affair in the press, in spite of her socialising.

Or not socialising.

His suspicions about that rang even louder now.

She turned around and he lifted his gaze. Her face was pink. He unsettled her. He couldn't deny a deep sense of satisfaction that he had such an effect on her. That he could ruffle that serene surface.

And nothing will ever come of it.

A lead weight settled in his belly.

Oblivious to his inner turmoil, Laia said, 'Thank you for that. I know you could have easily disabled me and let him know everything.'

Dax felt prickly, and it was directed at himself for being weak.

'I've never laid a hand on a woman in my life unless it was to bring pleasure. I'm not going to start now. And anyway, even if I had let him know where we were and he'd sent the cavalry, how am I meant to take you back? By force? You've made it clear that's not happening. I'll just have to wait for you to come to your senses.'

CHAPTER FOUR

'I'VE NEVER LAID *a hand on a woman in my life unless it* *was to bring pleasure.'*

Laia's brain was fused with white-hot heat at the thought of Dax's hands on her, bringing her pleasure.

She took a step backwards and said, a little breathlessly, 'I don't need to come to my senses. It's your brother who has to come to terms with the fact that he'll need to find a new royal bride.'

Dax shrugged. 'Why don't we agree to disagree for now?'

Laia didn't trust this amenability for a second. Maybe he'd decided to play some kind of *good cop* role so that he could play on her sense of guilt and persuade her she had no option but to agree to the marriage.

No way.

Her resolve firmed, Laia went to walk out of the media room.

She was almost at the door when he said from behind her, 'If you haven't already planned something, shall I look at what we can have for dinner?'

She turned around. Dax had his hands in the pockets of his board shorts. They hung low on his narrow hips. Together with the white polo shirt that made his skin look even darker, and his messy, overlong hair, he could have passed for a sexy pro-surfer or athlete—not a royal crown prince.

'You can cook?' she asked baldly.

'I'd hardly suggest it if I couldn't, would I?'

The man was full of surprises.

'That would be nice…if you don't mind. The larder and fridge are well-stocked. I need to take a shower.' She turned to leave, and then looked back at the last second. 'I— That is…you don't have to cook for me. We don't have to eat together.'

'You've ensured I'm stuck on this island with you for the foreseeable future. I think the least you can do is provide me with some company.'

Laia felt ridiculously gauche all of a sudden. 'Yes, of course. I meant, I just don't expect you to spend time with me if you'd prefer not to.'

A look flashed across his face—something that sparked a reaction deep inside her. An intense fluttering.

He said, 'I think that horse has bolted. Go and have your shower. I'll have the food ready when you come back.'

When Laia had dried off after her shower she considered her wardrobe, which was largely made up of casual wear, considering the location. She did have formal outfits—as she'd said to Dax, she had to be prepared for every eventuality. Anything could happen. She might be taken on a plane from here straight back to Isla'Rosa to deal with any amount of situations. She even had a funeral outfit. A black shift dress and matching jacket. Simple pearl jewellery.

But she usually veered away from black and thinking about death. She'd always felt as if grief had been embedded in her consciousness from birth, along with that sense of guilt and abandonment. Because it had coincided with the death of her mother.

She spotted a navy silk wrap maxi-dress and reached for it in a bid to divert her mind away from maudlin thoughts. Driven by a compulsion she didn't want to investigate—*to look pretty?*—she pulled it on over her underwear, tying the belt around her waist.

She tied her hair back in a loose knot to let the air get to her neck. It was cooler in the evenings, but no less stifling. She was about to put on some make-up, but stopped herself.

What was she doing? Making herself up for her prisoner?

A tiny semi-hysterical giggle rose up and she put a hand over her mouth. Hands down, this was the most outlandish thing she'd ever done in her life.

There was a sound from outside the dressing room and then a deep voice. 'Laia? Dinner is almost ready.'

She stepped out to see Dax in the doorway of her room. His gaze swept her up and down, from her bare feet to her face. A wave of heat followed his gaze.

'You look…lovely.'

Laia should be cursing herself, because now he would think she'd done this for him, but she couldn't seem to drum up the necessary recrimination.

'It's nothing special…it's just light and cool.'

Why did she sound so defensive?

Dax said, 'Why don't you go down? I've prepared you an aperitif. I'll have a quick shower and freshen up too.'

Feeling slightly as if she'd stepped into some parallel dimension, Laia watched Dax turn and leave. She locked her own bedroom door and put the key in its hiding place.

She went downstairs, curious as to what she'd find. First she noticed the delicious smell, and saw something simmering on the stove. She lifted the lid. It looked like a beef stew with vegetables and spices.

Then she noticed a glass with clear liquid and ice on the counter. And a slice of cucumber. She lifted it up and smelled it, her nose wrinkling slightly. She wasn't much of a drinker, and this definitely smelled alcoholic.

She tried it. Gin or vodka—she wasn't sure which. But it tasted refreshing and light.

She wandered over to the outside deck and looked out over the view. It never failed to take her breath away.

Dusk was falling into night. She could see the lights of the fishermen in their boats. She could see her own security team's boat. The two men were operating in shifts with another team. They would be quietly coming and going, being delivered to and from the bigger island, every couple of days.

The nights here always reminded her of velvet, because the warm air felt like a caress...

And then she heard a noise behind her and her skin prickled all over. She turned around. Dax had changed into dark trousers and a white shirt, sleeves rolled up, top button open. His hair was damp. Jaw clean-shaven. Feet bare. As were hers. For some reason that made her blood pulse. It felt intimate. When really, in this climate, it was just practical.

He looked very different from the rakish, messily gorgeous man she'd met after that polo match all those years ago, but no less sexy. More sexy, if anything. He was a man now. He'd lived. His body was honed and tightly muscled. Like a prize fighter.

'Laia, if you stare at me any harder I might explode.'

She blinked, and realised she was gripping the glass tightly. She relaxed. 'I was a million miles away.'

Dax put a hand to his chest. 'You *weren't* thinking about me?'

Laia fought down the rising flush. She took a sip of her drink and tried to appear nonchalant. 'Not everything is about you.'

She sat on a stool on the opposite side of the island and watched as Dax moved easily around the kitchen. Clearly at home there.

He said, with an edge to his tone, 'Oh, don't worry, I've known for a long time that it's not all about me.'

She knew immediately what he was talking about, and said quietly, 'You mean because you're the spare?'

He stopped in the middle of chopping a slice of cucumber for his own drink. Looked at her. 'You know, you're probably one of the few people in the world who would get that straight away.'

'I don't have a spare. It's all on me.'

Dax made a face and lifted his drink in her direction as a salute. 'Having a spare doesn't necessarily mean all that much difference. I never did the same classes as Ari. In many respects I'm not remotely prepared if something happens. It's as if just having a spare is enough.'

Laia remembered what it had been like, enduring endless lessons in stuffy rooms when it had been sunny outside.

'So you were separated at lot as children?'

'From the age of eight Ari was on a different schedule. There were weeks I hardly saw him. I was six.'

'You're obviously close…'

Dax took a sip of his drink. And then he said simply, 'I'd do anything for Ari.'

Laia felt her heart squeeze when she thought of Maddi and *her* selflessness. She said, 'I always wished for a sibling when I was growing up. I used to lie awake, worrying about what would happen if anything happened to me.'

'And yet here you are. Safe and well and about to be crowned Queen. But you're choosing not to make the process easier by marrying a man who is already King and who would help you carry the burden you've been carrying alone for years.'

Laia bristled. 'Maybe I don't want "easier". Maybe I don't want to marry a king who will automatically assume that role over a country he knows little about.'

'That's hardly his fault,' Dax pointed out. 'Even with the marriage agreement, and a thawing of relations between the two kingdoms, it's not as if things improved overnight. Hence this—'

Laia put up her hand. 'Don't say it.' She stood up from the stool, feeling agitated. 'I know how it looks for me to be flying in the face of what everyone must think is the logical solution. But I know my father wouldn't want to see Isla'Rosa become a suburb of Santanger. And with the best will in the world, that's what would happen.'

'You would be Queen of Santanger—you would have your own influence.'

Laia looked at Dax. 'I don't want to be Queen of Santanger. I just want to be Queen of Isla'Rosa. That's all I need.'

Dax was stirring the stew. He turned off the heat and turned around. 'And, according to you, *love*.'

Laia felt exposed again. 'Not necessarily love. I'm not that delusional.'

She wasn't going to admit to this man in a million years that she yearned for a soul-deep connection. He'd laugh his head off.

Laia sat back on the stool and said, 'I know it's not something that comes easily for people like us. What my mother and father had was rare and special.'

Dax frowned. 'They were in love?'

Laia nodded. 'My father adored my mother. He never married again.'

But he had an affair resulting in your secret half-sister.

Laia avoided Dax's eye. She could only imagine his cynical response if she told him about that. She didn't want Dax judging her father for his moment of weakness. A moment he'd never forgiven himself for.

Something about that caught at her, but Dax cut through her thoughts.

'If he'd married again—as I'm sure he was pressured to do—he might have had more children, given you siblings and some spares, taking some of the burden from you.'

Laia shifted uncomfortably on the stool. It was as if he *knew*. She felt the urge to blurt out the truth to Dax, in spite of how he might respond, and that made her wary. Very few people made her feel inclined to open up.

She held up her glass. 'Can I have another?'

Dax raised a brow and took her glass.

Laia saw his look and said defensively, 'It's nice, fresh. It doesn't really feel like drinking. I've never been drunk.'

'It's really not all it's cracked up to be.' Dax expertly and efficiently prepared another gin and tonic with fresh ice and a cucumber slice and handed it to her. 'Take it easy. I don't want to be responsible for getting you drunk for the first time. I don't know if my reputation can handle it.'

He seasoned the stew and then turned back.

'Speaking of reputations… You've managed to carve out quite a one for yourself, considering you've never been drunk.'

Laia nearly choked on her drink. She remembered seeing Dax in the club in Monte Carlo, when he'd said to her, *'We seem to frequent all the same social events and yet you're as elusive as the Scarlet Pimpernel.'*

She looked at him accusingly. 'You knew, didn't you?'

He shrugged. 'I think I realised after that night that something was up. It was the first time I'd seen you in the flesh on the circuit, even though we'd always both appear in the papers the next morning.'

'It wasn't the first time you'd seen me in the flesh, though...' Laia wasn't even sure where those words had come from. Falling out of her mouth before she could stop them.

Dax frowned. 'What do you mean? We'd never met before that night. Not face to face, at least.'

Laia felt a dart of hurt. She lifted her chin. 'It was in Paris...after a charity polo match. I was there with my father.'

He looked at her blankly for a long moment, and then slowly she could see the dawning of recognition. It was almost insulting.

'That was...years ago. You were a child.'

Obviously she wouldn't have interested him because she'd still been a teenager.

'It was eight years ago,' Laia said, too quickly. She cursed herself. 'I was sixteen. It's no wonder you don't remember.'

Dax grimaced slightly. 'My early twenties weren't my finest moments...a lot of that time is blurry. I re-call meeting your father briefly...' He looked at her and his eyes narrowed on her. 'And, yes, a young girl who looked very shy and—'

'That's okay. You don't have to say any more. That was me.' Even now Laia could remember the feeling of burning self-consciousness. The huge impact he'd had on her. That he still had on her. Mortifying. Why had she brought this up?

She wanted to drown in her drink and took a big gulp.

'You were much younger than everyone there. Then I realised who you were—Ari's fiancée.'

Laia glared at him. 'I was sixteen. I was no one's *fiancée.*'

He had the grace to wince. 'That does sound a little…weird. I used to tease Ari about being promised in marriage to a complete stranger.'

Dax was taking plates from a shelf and dishing up the stew, which smelled delicious. He was serving it with crusty bread.

He said, 'I've laid the table outside.'

Laia hadn't even noticed. She brought over the bread and Dax placed down the plates. He picked up a bottle of red wine and two glasses. There was a candle burning.

He sat down and Laia realised she was feeling a nice sensation of being cushioned against everything. Suddenly it didn't seem to matter that much that he only vaguely remembered her as an awkward teenager from that polo match in Paris.

He poured her some wine. She took a sip and asked, 'Why are you being so…calm about this? So…amenable?'

He sat down. 'Do you want to know the truth?'

She nodded and leant forward.

He leant forward too, and whispered. 'I haven't had a holiday in years.'

Laia sat back. She would have assumed he was on a permanent holiday—but then she thought of the conversation with his assistant. Montero Holdings. 'You see this as a holiday?'

'Why not? It's a tropical paradise. I have no devices to distract me. No idea what's going on in the outside world. I don't know when I'll have this chance again. I might as well make the most of it.'

Laia speared a morsel of succulent meat. 'You're making fun of me.'

'I swear to you I'm not. I've never been so cut off from everything and it's not that bad.'

Laia tasted the meat and almost closed her eyes. It was tender and tasty, with just the right amount of spiciness.

She put down her fork. 'Okay, how on earth did you learn to cook like that?'

'Aren't you being a little sexist? Where did *you* learn to cook? Neither of us grew up with expectations on us to cook or be domestic in any way.'

Laia put another forkful of food in her mouth to avoid answering.

When the silence grew taut between them Dax rolled his eyes and said, 'Okay, I'll go first. I went to a mixed sex boarding school in Switzerland for the last couple of years of high school. None of the boys took the cooking class because it was full of girls, but once I realised that I knew it was the class I wanted to be in. The guys laughed at me—but they weren't laughing when they realised I was the one with a girlfriend. And as it happens,' he went on, 'I turned out to have something of an affinity for cooking and baking.'

Laia put her fork down. She arched a brow. 'You bake too?'

'I make the most decadent chocolate cake.'

Laia couldn't quite believe what she was hearing—although she could well believe in Dax joining a class full of girls just to seduce them. That made sense.

She took another sip of wine, enjoying the velvety smoothness.

He gestured to her. 'What's your excuse?'

Laia was reluctant. This man made her feel so exposed. 'I feel like a bit of a fraud. I've got a very limited repertoire because I've only been learning in the last year…a friend has been teaching me.'

Dax raised a brow. 'A *male* friend?'

Laia blushed. 'No. A female friend.' *Her best friend. Maddi.* Impulsively she revealed, 'Apparently my mother was a good cook, so I always wanted to learn… But there never seemed to be the time and it wasn't considered appropriate.'

'Your mother died when you were born?'

She nodded, avoiding Dax's eye. She took another sip of wine. 'Just a few hours later.'

'That's tough…not to have known her.'

Laia felt ridiculously emotional. She forced it down and shrugged. 'You can't really miss what you never had.'

Except that was a lie, because she missed what she hadn't had almost every day.

She said huskily, 'My father was wonderful…at least I had him.'

Dax leaned over and topped up Laia's wine. 'My father was a serial philanderer. At least you didn't have to see something like that.'

She looked at Dax. She'd heard rumours over the years. Castle gossip. 'Did your mother know?'

He grimaced. 'You could say that. My father seemed to do it primarily to humiliate her. You see, she fell in love with him, and expected a relationship that my father had no interest in. So he punished her by showing her how weak she was for falling in love.'

Laia's mouth opened. She closed it. 'That's horrific. She must have been—'

'He destroyed her.' Dax cut her off. 'It destroyed her. Falling in love made her bitter and disappointed.'

Laia thought of Dax's tattoo. The caged bird.

'It sounds like your father's reaction to her loving him made her all those things.'

Laia remembered what people had whispered about Dax being responsible for his mother's death. Was that why he'd been sent off to boarding school? To get him away from the press and speculation?

'I'm sorry about your mother. You must have been young when she died.'

Dax took a healthy swallow of wine. 'Fifteen.'

She wondered if that had been around the time she'd first spied him in the distance at the palace in Santanger. She would have been only nine or ten. She had a vague memory of someone tall and gangly in the shadows. Had he been off the rails then? Was that what had led to his mother's death?

She didn't remember meeting the Queen—something about her not being well enough to receive them. She must have died not long afterwards.

Dax sat back and interrupted the buzz of questions in her head. 'So, why did you cultivate a very comprehensive fake persona of a party girl?'

Laia felt embarrassed now. As if she'd been caught playing dress-up. Reluctantly she admitted, 'I thought it would put your brother off.'

Dax sat back and made a small whistling noise. He let out a sharp laugh and then shook his head. 'You know what? I can see your logic… Ari is very straight. He has no time for frivolity.'

Laia made a face as if to say, *Right?*

But Dax shook his head again. 'You underestimated his stubbornness. That man is like a mule, and if he's set on a course of action then he won't stop until he gets what he wants.'

Laia shivered slightly, thinking of Maddi.

Dax sat forward. 'Are you cold?'

Laia shook her head. He was solicitous. She hadn't expected that. He'd been solicitous that night in the club in Monte Carlo… He'd put out his hand and touched her, and his touch had burned so much she'd pulled away like a frightened maiden.

Nothing had changed in the interim. She was still an innocent.

That burden sat like a stone in her gut. Suddenly her lofty ideals about love felt very naive and unattainable. Even if she did hold out for someone more compatible, how likely was it that there'd be the kind of passion she'd always dreamed of? The kind of passion she'd read about in the romance novels she'd hidden between the covers of the classics she'd speed-read in her English classes. The kind of passion that people said was unrealistic but she knew existed, deep in her bones, because she'd seen it. Smelled it. Ached for it.

This man looking at her now had awoken something inside her. A thirst. A hunger. That first face-to-face meeting with him had sparked such a visceral reaction that when he'd told her that one day he would be her brother-in-law she'd felt sick at the thought. Because how could this man who made her feel so many things, possibly ever be her brother? The idea had been horrifying…and so wrong.

Because she wanted him. She'd always wanted him.

Sitting at the table, Laia felt dizzy all of a sudden, as that revelation sank deep into her body, making her go hot and cold and hot again.

Dax was frowning now. 'Laia…?'

She stood up and swayed slightly, suddenly very aware that she'd reached her limit and gone past it.

Dax cursed and stood too. 'You've drunk too much.'

Laia wanted to laugh, but she was afraid she might be sick, because things were spinning a little.

She put a hand to her head. 'Maybe I should lie down for a minute.'

Dax came around the table. Before Laia knew what was happening he'd lifted her effortlessly into his arms and was carrying her through the villa.

This was worse. Far worse. Because now she was pressed against all that muscle and sinew. His scent was all around her and infiltrating her blood, making it warm. Her dress was no barrier to his heat and the steely strength of his body. Her breasts were pressed against his chest. Her face was so close to his neck. If she moved her head forward even just a tiny bit she could press her lips against his skin.

They were at her bedroom door. Laia blinked. Had she really drunk that much? Dax put her down, and thankfully she didn't sway again. The spinning sensation had calmed down.

His voice was tight. 'Do you have the key to your room?'

Laia nodded. 'You'll have to turn around so you don't know where it's kept.'

Dax's jaw clenched, but he turned around. His shoulders looked so broad, and he was so tall. The fuzziness from the alcohol was starting to wear off and she realised she was staring at Dax's back like a lovestruck groupie.

She turned quickly and took the key from its hiding spot and opened her door, slipping inside.

Dax turned around. 'Are you going to be okay?'

Laia nodded, but her head swam a bit again so she stopped. 'Fine. Thank you for dinner. It was really good.'

'You're welcome.'

'Goodnight, Dax.'

She was closing the door when he put a hand on it.

'I'd feel a lot better if you left your door open tonight.'

Laia had all her devices—phone and laptop—locked away in a safe. So there was no real reason to lock her door.

She stood back and held the door open. 'Okay, fine.'

After a long few seconds Dax backed away. 'Call me if you need anything.'

He turned and left and Laia felt very discombobulated. Who was the captor here and who was the captee?

The effects of the alcohol seemed to be fading as quickly as they'd surfaced. Maybe it hadn't been the alcohol at all, but the massive and unwelcome revelation that she really didn't want to look at.

So she didn't.

She changed into her night shorts and tank top and washed her face, and then climbed into bed. The room revolved alarmingly for a moment, but mercifully stopped after a few seconds. And then she fell asleep.

A little later, Dax stopped by Laia's open bedroom door. The muslin net around her bed was still tied up, so she wasn't being protected from biting insects.

Telling himself that he was just doing her a favour, and also delivering a big glass of water, Dax went in and put the water down on the bedside table.

Laia didn't stir. She was on her back. One arm over her chest. Dark hair spread out around her head. It tended towards the wild and wavy. He liked it. It hinted at other depths beneath the largely serene surface she projected—or had been taught to project.

He recognised it from his brother Ari. They would both have been taught at an early age not to show emotion.

And yet when he'd been telling her about his mother, just a short while before—something he avoided talking about at all costs, usually—Laia's eyes had filled with compassion.

Dax diverted his mind from how that had made him feel. He didn't ask for an emotional response from anyone.

The light sheet was pushed down to Laia's waist. One long leg was sticking out. She wore a tank top that did little to hide the firm swells of her breasts.

He could still feel them pressed against his chest as he'd carried her to the bedroom. She'd felt so light in his arms, but strong too. He'd felt her breath on his neck…warm.

By the time he'd put her on her feet his blood had been clamouring for *more*. To touch her. Explore that lithe body. Feel her under his mouth. Opening to him.

Cursing under his breath now, Dax moved silently around the bed, drawing the protective net down. This woman could not be his. No matter what she said, she was destined to be Queen of Santanger. He knew his brother, and Ari would stop at nothing to have his Queen by his side.

Dax would not betray his trust. But it might kill him in the process.

When Laia woke she was disorientated. She cracked open an eye and all she saw was fuzziness—until she realised it was the mosquito net around the bed. It was dawn outside, so mercifully it wasn't too hot yet.

She came up on one elbow and winced when her brain collided with her head. Her mouth felt as dry as sandpaper. She spied a glass of water by the bed and pulled back the net to get it.

Had she brought that up to bed? She couldn't recall. Last night wasn't a blank but it was a bit blurry. She took a big gulp of water. She recalled talking to Dax for ages. About things that she hadn't expected at all. Or had that all been a dream?

He'd told her about his parents.

He could cook like a pro.

So unexpected.

Laia got out of bed and went to the bathroom. Her hair was a big tangle around her shoulders. She couldn't look less like a crown princess right now. The stuffy Privy Council would be horrified.

As she went back towards the bed she passed her open door, leading out to the corridor. Dax's room was on the other side of the hall. Laia found her feet taking her out of her room and down the hall.

Dax's door was wide open.

So he would have heard her if she'd felt ill during the night?

She crept closer. His room was dark—it was on the west side of the villa so the sun would hit her room first.

Knowing she was intruding, but unable to stop herself, Laia went further into the room. His net was pulled around the bed, but there was a chink between two ends that was open.

It gave her a perfect view of the man on the bed. And he was naked. Laia's feet were stuck to the floor. The sheet had been thrown off completely and Dax lay in a sprawl, one leg bent. One hand was on his chest, which rose and fell rhythmically.

He was breathtaking. That was the only word to describe it. Every muscle clearly delineated. Not a spare ounce of flesh. Corded muscles on his legs. His narrow waist. And...

Laia's breath stopped when her gaze rested on the potent centre of his masculinity.

She'd never seen a naked man in the flesh before. She knew she was transgressing a million boundaries and invading Dax's space, but she couldn't look away.

Even at rest he was impressive. Intimidating. Laia wondered what it must be like to lie next to a man like this. To wake up beside him. To have permission to touch him when you wanted because he was *yours*. To wrap your hand around—

Dax shifted on the bed and Laia froze in terror, her gaze on his face now, imagining his eyes opening. Those too-blue eyes fixing on her. Finding her ogling him. But they didn't open.

Laia backed away from the bed, the net obscuring her vision again. And then she turned around and fled, straight back to her room, closing the door silently behind her. She was wide awake now. She didn't think she'd ever get that image of Dax erased from her brain. *And she didn't want to.*

He was beautiful. She couldn't deny it. She wanted Dax. She'd wanted him from the moment she'd laid eyes on him.

And now he was here.

The moment she left this place she would become Queen of Isla'Rosa and her life would not be hers again. She would have to deal with the fallout of not marrying King Aristedes and, once that had passed, everyone would be preoccupied with who she *would* be marrying.

She knew that even if she found someone she could consider a soulmate, someone who could be her companion throughout her life as Queen, she might never experience the kind of passion that she'd dreamed of. That she felt instinctively could be experienced with a man like Dax.

An audacious thought occurred to her.

He's a crown prince...eminently suitable for me to marry.

Laia's heart thumped.

But no. Crown Prince Dax of Santanger had made

it very clear that his destiny was not his brother's—settling down and begetting heirs. He would be completely unsuitable. How could she even trust a man like that?

No, she didn't want him for marriage. She wanted him for something else. For something very selfish. For *her*. She wanted to know what real passion felt like before she had to settle down and live a life of duty and responsibility. Because her people would always come first. They had to.

Dax had haunted her for years. She was only realising how much now, here in this lush paradise, when she could no longer hide from herself and her desires. He didn't disgust her at all. The opposite.

Seduce him.

No. Ridiculous. Nonsensical. She didn't have the skills or the wherewithal to seduce an expert connoisseur of women. She wouldn't even know where to start… She could already feel the humiliation if she made herself vulnerable and he rejected her. He'd probably do it with kindness, which would be so much worse.

Laia started to pace. But the suggestion wouldn't fade as it should. Because surely there was no way.

If you seduce him then he will know you're serious about not wanting to marry King Aristedes.

Laia stopped pacing. Could she really be considering this? The prospect of pitting Dax against his brother… by using herself?

It wouldn't work. She wasn't so irresistible. She wasn't even sure if he wanted her. Maybe she was just imagining it when she thought she felt his eyes on her. When she thought she felt something pulse between them, alive and electric… He was a man—he was just reacting to her as a woman.

Well, then, if it won't work, what have you got to lose?

CHAPTER FIVE

A COUPLE OF hours later Laia was making breakfast. She felt on edge at the thought of trying to seduce Dax. It was almost as crazy a notion as keeping him captive on this island.

And how on earth did a virgin go about seducing one of the world's most renowned and discerning lovers? What did he feel for her? Anything? He was so hard to read.

When he appeared at that moment, with damp hair and a freshly shaven jaw, she nearly jumped out of her skin.

'Okay?' he asked.

'Fine…just…you startled me.'

He was wearing board shorts and a short-sleeved shirt, open at the top. He looked irritatingly relaxed. And gorgeous.

Her head was unhelpfully filled with images of him sprawled naked on the bed. Her cheeks grew warm.

She said quickly, 'Thank you…for last night. The glass of water. I'm sure I could have made it to bed without being carried, but…'

It was nice.

She shut her mouth quickly, and then said, 'I'm making breakfast omelettes, if you'd like one?'

'I would love one, thank you. Is there anything I can do?'

'You could make the coffee?'

Dax moved around behind her and Laia fumbled with the eggs on the pan, cursing herself silently. She managed to make two fluffy omelettes, in spite of her jitters, and carried them over to the table on two plates.

Dax had poured two coffees and brought over orange juice, bread and pastries.

Laia had only just got used to spending time with Maddi, her half-sister, in the last year. Until she'd met Maddi, she'd had quite a lonely existence, surrounded by people all the time but never in an intimate space.

That was what had made her even more determined not to marry King Aristedes. He would be as important and as busy as her. He'd been so dismissive of her all along that she could envisage a marriage where they lived parallel lives, only coming together for the necessary conjugal relations.

'Another beautiful day for a prisoner in paradise.' Dax lifted his glass of orange juice in a little mocking salute.

Laia said, 'Another week at the most and you'll have your freedom back.'

She thought of him going back out into the world and resuming his carefree existence. Being photographed with beautiful women at the opening of every glitzy event. Could she really do this and deal with *that*?

Yes, because then she'd be able to move on.

Wasn't that how it worked? That was how men said it worked—once you'd had what you wanted you were sated.

Laia sat back and cradled her coffee cup in her hand. Curiosity got the better of her. 'So what's your story? You don't have the same pressure as Aristedes to settle down and have heirs…but will you marry?'

He looked at her. 'I hope that's not a proposal, because you're already engaged.'

Laia scowled at him. 'You know that's not what I meant.'

He wiped his mouth and put down his fork. 'That's a very personal question.'

'Well, seeing as how you're so determined for me to become your sister-in-law, maybe we should get better acquainted.' He couldn't argue against that.

His eyes narrowed, but she just smiled sweetly. His gaze dropped to her mouth and lingered. Laia's smile faded. He looked up, blinked. Her pulse tripped and settled on a faster rhythm. Warmth filled her lower body.

Then the charged moment was gone. He sat back. 'I have no intention of settling down. That's my brother's domain.'

So far exactly what she'd surmised herself.

Laia took a sip of coffee. 'What do you have against it?'

'Nothing. It's just not for me. It's not something I've ever envisaged.'

'I guess I'm not surprised to hear you say that.'

'And why would that be?' he asked, civilly enough. But she heard the thread of steel underneath. She felt as if she was skirting round the edges of something potentially fiery.

'Your…er…way of life seems to back up what you say. You don't seem inclined to sacrifice your independence any time soon. Although there are questions in the media as to why you haven't been seen for some time…'

'You've been looking me up online?'

'It doesn't take much for headlines about Prince Dax to appear at the top of any search feed.'

'Not that it's any business of—anyone's.'

He said this with a definite edge, which made Laia wonder who had said something to him—perhaps Aristedes?

He continued, 'I've been busy. With work.'

Laia tapped a nail against the side of her cup as something occurred to her. She watched his reaction as she said, 'I'm not sure if I'm the only one who likes to hide behind a certain…persona.'

Dax went very still. 'What's that supposed to mean?'

'You weren't drunk that night in Monte Carlo.'

'I haven't been drunk in years. I told you—it's overrated.'

'And yet you were there…on the scene. And I know how tedious it can be if you're not on the same energetic level as everyone else. Which is why I could never last long.'

'Maybe I was on drugs?'

Laia shook her head. 'I don't think so. You didn't have that glazed, manic look. No, I think you were doing exactly the same thing as me. You were doing your work behind the scenes while faking a façade… Why, though?'

* * *

Dax's jaw clenched. He wasn't used to this much conversation in the mornings—generally because he wasn't ever with women in the mornings. It wasn't unpleasant…but he didn't like being on the other end of scrutiny. Especially not Laia's particular brand of very perspicacious scrutiny.

He shrugged. 'Maybe, like you, I had my reasons. When people underestimate you, it gives you an edge over them.'

'But that only lasts as long as the first time. Once people know they've underestimated you it won't happen again.'

Dax arched a brow. 'You'd be surprised.'

'You run a business—Montero Holdings?'

He nodded. 'It's a software business.'

'Is that something you were into at school? How did you cope with your dyslexia?'

Before Dax could answer, she blushed.

'Sorry, I ask too many questions.'

The colour staining her cheeks made him want to touch her there, to see if her skin felt hot. He forced himself to focus.

'School was…a challenge. Until they figured out what the problem was. There was an assumption that I just wasn't that bright.'

Her green eyes were wide and filled with compassion. Dax put it down to an automatic reflex. Ari had that ability too—to be able to make people feel that he really cared.

She asked, 'How did you cope until they realised what it was?'

Dax shook off the pricking of his conscience, mocking his cynicism for judging Laia's compassion to be fake. Maybe he couldn't handle real compassion.

Maybe he didn't want to. Because that would be like allowing a chink of light into an area he liked to keep shut away. The place where he held his guilt and toxic memories of the past...where he didn't feel he deserved compassion.

He forced that out of his head and said, 'When I went to a conventional school for those final years they caught it almost immediately. They're much better now at recognising the signs and accommodating students who are dyslexic. I had learnt to navigate around it. That's how I realised I was good at computers. Not the coding so much, but an overall vision of system designs.'

Laia said nothing for a moment, and Dax realised that she often did that. She didn't necessarily fill a gap in the conversation with chatter. He liked it.

She put her head on one side. 'You're global, aren't you? Your company supplies software systems for us in Isla'Rosa.'

Dax nodded. 'We most likely do. We're one of the biggest software design companies in the world.'

'And you're on the board of that charity. There's no way you'd be on the board if you weren't pulling your weight.'

Dax felt a little exposed. 'It's a cause close to my heart.'

'Why?'

'I have empathy for kids whose lives are torn apart,

who look around and find everything they knew is gone…everyone they knew.'

Dax thought back to the aftermath of the car crash, when his entire world had seemed to splinter into a thousand pieces. The crash had pulled back the curtain on the fallacy that they'd all been living a relatively functional existence.

Or it would have if he hadn't decided to do something that would protect his mother and her secrets for ever from the vultures who'd been circling. A decision that had defined his existence for a long time. *Still did.* Guilt was a canny operator.

Laia was looking at him, waiting for him to elaborate. Ordinarily he wouldn't feel inclined to, but now he did.

'The car crash that killed my mother was a pretty shattering experience. It exposed a lot of the flaws in our family. On the surface it looked perfect. But it wasn't. It was toxic. Ari was busy learning how to be King. Our father was busy parading his various mistresses in front of our mother, sending her slowly over the edge. And I… I was the only one she could turn to.'

Dax expected Laia to ask more about the crash, but she said, 'Is that why you don't want to marry?'

'It's part of it. I didn't see anything good in my parents' marriage. They certainly weren't like your parents. In love.'

Laia was quiet for a moment, and then she blurted out, 'My father had an affair.'

Dax raised a brow, glad to have the focus turned from him.

Laia continued. 'It was a year after my mother died, I was still a baby.'

'Who was she?'

'She was one of the castle staff. But then she got pregnant. My father panicked and sent her into exile. He felt so guilt-ridden. Like he'd tainted my mother's memory. I think that's why he never married again. It was some sort of penance.'

'What happened to the baby? Your half-sibling?'

Laia swallowed. 'A half-sister, actually.'

'Have you met her?'

Laia nodded. She looked guilty.

Dax narrowed his gaze on her. 'Laia, what—?'

'She's in Santanger...with Aristedes. That's Maddi—my half-sister.'

Dax's mouth closed. Opened. Closed again. He thought of the pictures he'd seen. Eventually he said, half to himself, 'That's why you look so alike. You're sisters.' Then he asked, 'Whose idea was it?'

'Maddi thought of it...but I went along with it. It was both of us.'

Dax thought of his brother, finding out that Princess Laia wasn't who he thought she was. Finding out that he had an imposter in his palace. Feeling like a fool.

Anger rose, and Dax told himself it was because of *this* and not because sitting here talking to Laia was like finding himself in a confessional, blithely spilling his guts after years of keeping them firmly tucked away from sight.

He said, with bite, 'How noble of you not to blame her entirely for duping my brother, making him look like a fool.'

Laia's hands twisted her napkin, belying what? Her guilt?

'It seems like no one is any the wiser about who Maddi really is,' she said, her tone a little defiant. 'And he's using her to make it look like all is well with the engagement, so who's duping who?'

'That's not the same. All he can do is damage limitation, thanks to you.'

Laia put down her napkin. 'If he'd listened to me back when I tried to talk to him we wouldn't even be in this situation, but his arrogance has brought us here.'

Dax stood up abruptly. He needed to get away from those big green eyes. Her gaze was too direct.

'I'm going for a walk.'

He needed to put some distance between them. Maybe then he could get some oxygen to his brain to assess what she'd just told him.

And what you told her...practically everything.

Laia watched Dax walk out, his tall, powerful body vibrating with tension. He was angry. And she couldn't blame him after finding out the extent of how she and her sister had tricked King Aristedes.

If anything, Dax's loyalty to his brother showed yet another facet to his personality, which was evolving into something Laia had no handle on any more.

She'd thought she'd had him all sized up. In a box marked *Playboy Reprobate*.

But—as the headlines had alluded to—was he that any more? Was he changing?

She had to admit that he had far more substance than she'd given him credit for. A self-made billionaire in his own right, apart from any royal inheritance. And he'd done all that while being dyslexic—an added challenge.

Laia cleared up the breakfast detritus. Dax had disappeared somewhere into the thick foliage of the forest. No doubt cursing her with every step. So far, her plan to seduce the man was going very well. Right now, he couldn't stand her.

Brava, Laia.

She dumped the plates into the sink to wash later, and went up to her bedroom to take part in a scheduled online meeting with her advisors in Isla'Rosa. Perhaps she'd do better to focus on the very big stuff coming down the tracks—like being crowned Queen of Isla'Rosa—rather than fantasising about seducing a man way out of her league.

Dax was still angry, and now frustrated. He pushed leaves aside as he powered down yet another path. Thick foliage lined the track. Sweat was springing from every part of his skin in the humidity. He had no idea where he was heading, but he figured he couldn't get too lost because the island was small.

He eventually emerged at a small sandy beach. Its serene beauty distracted him for a moment, before he remembered to stay angry. And not to think about Laia's big green eyes. Or the expression of contrition he'd seen in them even though she'd sounded defiant.

He pulled off his sneakers and sat down on the sand under the shade of a tree.

The problem was, he was angry for his brother—of course. Ari didn't deserve this. His whole life had been dedicated to the service of his—*their*—country. And supporting Dax.

After the car accident that had killed their mother, it had been as if Ari had known that Dax needed space to get away from Santanger and what had happened. The awful tragedy, his part in it, and all the toxicity that had led to it.

Ari had persuaded their father to let Dax finish school abroad. And then a year later their father had died and it had been just the two of them. By some unspoken agreement, once Dax had graduated from high school Ari had let him carve out a life away from Santanger.

Only Ari had known the full extent of all that Dax had to carry, and Dax had known his brother felt guilty. For not noticing more. For not being there. Even though he'd had his own huge burden to carry. Taking on the weight of the crown.

But that was why Ari had let Dax have his freedom. It had been a tacit form of asking forgiveness.

So Dax had gone away. For a few years he had lived a hedonistic life as the Playboy Prince. Carousing to escape his memories and the past. But it hadn't lasted half as long as people thought it had.

He'd grown bored with it quickly—but then he'd realised that he could use it to his advantage. When people underestimated him—and that was most people, most of the time—he used it against them.

In the process he'd built up a global empire. But lately he'd had to come to terms with the fact that his reputation wasn't doing him any favours any more.

His time playing the playboy was coming to an end,

and for the first time Dax wasn't sure which way to go. Ari had the kingdom and his upcoming marriage. Even if it wasn't to Laia, it would be to someone. He would be creating a new life and the next generation.

Dax knew his anger wasn't just for his brother being made a fool. It was more complicated. It was anger at himself, for wanting a woman he couldn't have.

The way Laia had looked at him just a short while before, asking questions that cut right to the heart of who he was and his *modus operandi*, had not been expected...or welcome.

'So what's your story? Will you marry?' she'd asked. As impertinently as...as a queen would.

It was rare for Dax to meet someone who was his equal in the way she was. In terms of social standing, as afforded to them by an accident of birth, but also in terms of experience.

They'd both grown up in their respective bubbles of royal courts. With great privilege. A mix of home schooling and other exclusive establishments with the children of presidents and the wealthiest people on the planet.

It was a world Dax was inextricably bound with and to, and yet he'd distanced himself from it in many ways. But, no matter what he did or where he went, he would always be Crown Prince Dax. The spare to the heir. The bad boy to Ari's good boy. A reputation he'd created and cultivated but which was beginning to feel more and more restrictive.

The burden would lift slightly once Ari had heirs and they took on the Crown Prince or Crown Princess title.

'Will you marry?'

Dax shuddered at the thought, his mind flooded with memories of his father parading his latest mistress through the palace while his mother screamed and wept in her rooms. Make-up running down her ravaged face. Breath smelling of gin. Eyes glazing over as she eventually calmed down and the medication the doctors had given her did their work in her blood system.

Dax had hated those doctors for coming in and giving her so many pills, because he'd seen the way she disappeared and became pliant. Quiet. But she'd wanted the pills. Needed them. More and more. Until she hadn't been able to get through a day without them.

Ari had come in one day after she'd had a hysterical bout and he'd looked horrified. 'What's wrong with her?'

Dax had felt guilty—as if it was his fault she was in such a state. As if he should somehow stop it. He hadn't had the appetite to tell Ari that this was how she was nearly every day. Nothing unusual. And he was the one she wanted by her side. Consoling her. Listening to her.

She'd tell him over and over again, *'Never give away your heart, Dax, they don't want it. They'll take it out and crush it to pieces in front of you...in front of everyone.'*

The silence was broken only by the call of birds, insects, and the waves gently breaking on the shore. It was hot and getting hotter.

Feeling claustrophobic after the onslaught of unwelcome memories, Dax stood up and started to strip off until he was naked. And then he walked into the sea, letting its relative cool wash over him and suck him under, where he could try and drown out the fact that he was stuck here with a woman who was simultaneously bringing back the past in a way that was most unwelcome while driving him insane with lust.

Not a good combination.

Laia emerged onto the beach from the treeline. She saw Dax's clothes on the sand. No sign of the man. She shaded her eyes and looked out to sea. She still couldn't see him.

A knot formed in her gut as she scanned the horizon, until finally she saw a speck in the distance. The knot loosened marginally as the speck got larger as he swam back to shore. Had he been trying to escape? Or just swimming…?

She went down to the shoreline, dropping her things as she did. She wore a one-piece swimsuit under a floaty kaftan that came to her thighs.

She could see Dax's powerful arms now, scissoring rhythmically in and out of the water. Eventually he was close enough to stand. The water lapped around his chest. His messy hair was slicked back and dark. He saw her, and she noticed the tension coming into his body.

'How did you find me?'

Laia's gut clenched. She felt as if she was intruding. He hadn't wanted her to find him. And why would he? She'd incarcerated him here and he'd just found out she had a half-sister who was pretending to be her.

'You set off the alarms.'

Dax splashed water onto his face, and then said, 'Well? Are you going to stand there all day or get in?'

Laia felt ridiculously awkward. And self-conscious. She told herself she was being ridiculous. This man had been to yacht parties where women cavorted with little else but a piece of string protecting their modesty.

She looked away and pulled off her kaftan. How on earth was she going to seduce this man if she couldn't even bare herself in a one-piece swimsuit in front of him?

She threw the kaftan onto the ground, annoyed with herself now, and stepped into the water until it reached her waist. And then she dived under, hoping for a graceful surfacing near Dax, but she swallowed some water and emerged coughing and spluttering.

He was grinning. 'Okay?'

Laia nodded, regaining her composure, treading water. It was like cool silk against her skin. This was her favourite place to come for a swim.

'Look,' she said, 'I'm sorry for all this, but I truly believe I have no choice but to see this through now to the end.'

'Sorry enough to let me go?'

Laia was struck by a pang. He wanted to get away from her. Apart from anything else, she hadn't expected it to be so easy to talk to him. To tell him things.

She shook her head. 'I'm sorry, no. Not yet.'

Dax didn't look surprised. He said, 'I need to check in with my assistant John.'

Laia nodded. 'I can arrange that.'

'I'm going to get out now.'

'Okay…' Laia wondered why he was telling her this. And then he said, 'You might want to turn around.'

'Why?'

'Because I'm naked.'

Even though she was in the cool water, heat flooded Laia all the way up to her cheeks. 'Oh, right…of course.'

She turned to face out to the horizon. She could hear Dax moving through the water back to shore. Unable to help herself, she turned her head just as he was walking out through the shallows.

His body gleamed. Strong, broad back. Narrow waist. Powerful buttocks, high and firm, those long legs.

Before she knew what was happening, he'd stopped and looked back, his body now in profile to her. It took Laia long seconds to realise that he was looking at her looking at him. Avidly.

She whirled around and ducked under the water in a bid to hide what she'd been doing. So fast that she swallowed water again and had to come up for air, gasping.

She wasn't sure, but she could have sworn she heard an evil chuckle from the beach.

Dax was sitting on the beach, dressed again, with his shirt hanging open. Laia couldn't put off coming out of the water any longer. She was acutely conscious of the way the material of her swimsuit clung to every inch of her body. It had felt conservative when she'd put it on, but now it felt as if it was indecently cut. Too high on her thighs. And low over her chest.

As she splashed out of the shallows she tried not to imagine that he was comparing her to every other woman he'd seen similarly dressed.

'You didn't have to wait,' she told him.

'I couldn't risk you getting a cramp and having that on my conscience. Some of us do have a conscience, you know.'

Laia grabbed her kaftan, but at the last second didn't pull it on. She sat down on the warm sand next to Dax.

She made a snorting sound. 'I'm sure there are legions of women all over the world who might argue that.'

'You're insinuating I treat women badly? I'm wounded.'

Laia squinted at him. The sun was high. 'With the best will in the world, some of them must have wanted…more? And been disappointed.'

'That might well have been the case…but I have never given any lover false hope. They always knew where they stood.'

Laia had to admit she believed him. But she was curious to know how it could be with a man like this.

'And where was that?' she asked.

'In something purely fun and physical for as long as we wanted each other.'

'Which was how long?'

He looked at her. And then he seemed to consider his answer before he said, 'Never longer than a few dates.'

Imagine capturing this man's attention even just for a few dates…

'What would happen if they wanted more?'

'I would end it.'

No hesitation. Stark. Absolute.

'You never found yourself transgressing your own boundaries?'

He shook his head emphatically. 'Never.'

For some reason this made Laia feel slightly giddy. And then she sobered. She didn't want to be the one to engage Dax's emotions. She only wanted him for one thing. Well, two. Passion and sex.

And then he completely took the wind out of her sails when he said, 'What about you?'

Laia's insides tightened. 'What about me, what?'

'How do you treat your lovers?'

Laia felt sure he was making fun of her. He had to know… But he was just looking at her with a curious expression.

She shrugged as nonchalantly as she could, 'Oh, you know… I make it clear that I'm not up for anything serious…how can I be?'

'Because you're engaged.'

Laia scowled at him, but was grateful for the diversion. 'No, because very soon I'll be crowned Queen and I have a life of duty ahead of me.'

'You'll have to marry and have heirs, whether it's to Ari or someone else of royal lineage.'

'Yes, I'm aware of that. But my husband will be my choice.'

'Why won't you just *do* this?'

There was an edge to Dax's voice that Laia felt deep inside. His frustration was evident. It made her prickly.

She turned to face him, trying to make him understand. 'Because if I marry Aristedes then Isla'Rosa becomes a suburb of Santanger, no matter how he might deny it. We've carved out our independence and identity after years of conflict—'

'Exactly,' interjected Dax. 'Wouldn't this bring peace once and for all?'

Laia shook her head. 'Not at the cost of our independence. It's too much. I want to lead our people out of the past and into a modern, bright future. I know that's going to be a challenge, but I can do it. My path is side by side with Santanger, not as a part of it. Peace is possible through other routes.'

Dax just looked at her, and Laia hated it that it mattered to her that he *got* it. She sensed that he sympathised with where she was coming from, but his loyalty to his brother trumped his own instincts. He was loyal to his brother, not to her, and that made total sense so why did it matter?

Because you already care what he thinks of you. You want his loyalty.

That incendiary thought drove Laia to her feet, her kaftan gripped in her hand.

'Look, Dax, you've abdicated your responsibilities—for whatever reason. You live your life from day to day, free to choose what you want when you want, with no one dictating to you how you're to live your life. You just don't get it. How can you?'

Laia went to walk away, but before she could take two steps Dax's hand was around her arm and he was whirling her back to face him. His face was like thunder.

'What the hell is that supposed to mean?'

Laia gulped. But not out of pain. Dax was barely holding her arm. It was because he was suddenly so close. And he was bristling.

'Abdicated my responsibilities?'

Laia pulled her arm free. Weakly, she said, 'I don't know what arrangement you have with your brother, but it's not as if you live a life full of royal duty.'

Dax's mouth was thin. 'No, you *don't* know anything about our arrangement, Princess. Maybe I had responsibilities that you know nothing about. Responsibilities that meant my brother got to focus on his job without being burdened by—' He stopped abruptly.

Laia wanted to ask, *Burdened by what?* But she kept her mouth shut. She wondered if he was talking about his mother.

'The way I live my life is none of your concern,' he said. 'Or anyone else's. Except maybe my brother's.'

Laia couldn't look away from Dax's eyes. They were so blue it hurt. They should have been icy, but she felt warm. And it wasn't the sun or the humidity.

She knew she should leave this alone, but words were spilling out before she could censor them. 'Did something happen? So Aristedes allowed you to walk away…?'

Dax's face tightened. His voice was a growl. 'Leave it alone, Laia, you have no idea what you're talking about.'

But it was there in his eyes, deep inside. Incredible pain. His whole body was vibrating with tension.

Without even realising what she was doing she moved closer. She'd dropped the kaftan to the sand… hadn't even noticed.

Dax said warningly, 'Laia—'

She put her hand on his bare chest. Exactly as she'd wanted to the other day. Dax's eyes flared. He put his hand over hers. But he didn't pull her hand away.

His skin was warm. Still damp from the sea. She could feel his heart. Strong and steady. Maybe a little fast. Like hers. His hand felt huge, enveloping hers.

'Laia, what are you doing?'

Her eyes fell to his mouth. It wasn't thin any more. It was lush and full. She frowned, her mind not able to let go the strand of thought it had just been picking at, in spite of Dax's warnings.

She asked, 'What happened to make your brother give you a life of freedom?'

She looked up as something occurred to her. He must have seen it in her eyes, because before she could say another word Dax had snaked his free hand under her wet hair and around to the back of her neck.

And then his mouth was on hers, and Laia didn't have any thoughts in her head any more. Because they were incinerated by the fire.

CHAPTER SIX

DAX HADN'T INTENDED to kiss Laia. Yet here he was, mouth fused to hers, and he'd never felt anything so erotically charged. She was everything he'd imagined—*fantasised*—and more.

She was soft and yet hard at the same time. Her hand was curled into his over his chest. He burned where she'd put her hand over his heart. No one had ever touched him like that. Her breasts were crushed to his chest. When had they moved so close that he could feel every inch of her lithe, supple body?

Her other arm crept around his neck. Dax desperately tried to claw back some sense of control, some coherence around why he was doing this, but it was impossible. It had something to do with needing to make her stop talking…stop looking at him as if she could see all the way down to his deepest darkest shadows.

She was lush and sweet and hesitant and bold all at once. Her mouth opened under his and Dax was lost, drowning, spinning into infinity. He'd kissed women. Many, many women. Not as many as people thought, but a lot. Enough to know that this kiss was unlike any other.

It beat through him like a drum: *his, his, his.*

He wanted this woman. He wanted to taste every inch of her and he wanted to sink so deep inside her that she would be ruined for all other men.

A klaxon went off in his brain—*she's not yours to ruin!*

Dax jerked his head backwards so fast he felt dizzy. Laia opened her eyes. They looked unfocused. Her mouth was swollen. They were still welded together— chest, thighs, hips. His body was aching and hard, pressing against her soft belly.

Dax put his hands on her arms and took a step back, pushed her away from him.

Laia blinked. 'What was that?'

'That,' Dax said grimly, 'was a mistake.'

Laia was still trying to process what had just happened. An earthquake? But the island seemed fine. The sea was calm. *No.* The earthquake had happened inside her. One minute she'd been standing there, looking at Dax, and the next…the next she'd been consumed.

She could still feel his mouth on hers, *hard.* His body against hers, *hard.* She grew warm when she registered exactly how hard…pressed against her belly.

She'd imagined that kiss her whole life. That was the kiss of her dreams and fantasies. Yet it had burnt her imaginings to dust. She'd never expected to feel so full of fire. So full of earthy lustiness. She'd never expected to feel that ache in her lower body. That pooling of heat between her legs. The way her breasts had felt heavy and tight.

Dax was holding something out to her. She looked at it. Her kaftan.

He said, 'Please, put this on.'

Laia felt uncoordinated as she took it and tried to figure out where the arm and head holes were. She heard a curse, and then seconds later Dax had stepped closer and was putting it over her head.

Laia, ridiculously, felt like giggling at Dax's stern expression. He was helping her find the armholes now and threading her arms through. The light, diaphanous material settled around her body, covering her.

Then he started striding back up the beach towards the trees.

Laia called out, 'Where are you going?'

He threw over his shoulder, 'Back to the villa.'

Laia realised at that moment that her legs were like jelly. She sank down onto the sand. She just needed a moment to assimilate different things.

Dax wanted her.

She'd felt it.

She was sure it was just a consequence of his being stuck on this island with her…he was a highly sexed man. But her plan to seduce him didn't look so ridiculous any more. At least she knew he wanted her.

She sat there in a semi stupor for long minutes. Rendered insensible by a kiss. A mere kiss. It was pathetic, really. But it was also glorious. The culmination of all her ardent longings since she'd laid eyes on him that first time in Paris. And it had surpassed anything her fevered brain could have imagined.

She visualised Dax coming back down to check on

her and finding her here like this—wrecked after a kiss—and scrambled to her feet.

.She tried to reduce the significance of what had just happened as she walked back. It had just been the culmination of years of longing for something—if Dax kissed her again surely it wouldn't have the same effect?

But just the thought of Dax kissing her again made Laia almost miss her footing on the path. She cursed softly. She had to get it together. She had a job to do. Seduce Dax, and in the process make it crystal-clear that she would never be marrying his brother.

And then put Dax and the past behind her and get on with her life. A life on her terms.

Dax was coming down to the kitchen level after taking a long, cold shower when Laia returned from the beach. She looked like a sexy sea nymph, with her hair in a wild sea salt tangle around her shoulders and skin burnished from the sun. Bare feet.

At least she was wearing the kaftan, which covered her body from throat to thigh. But even in spite of that he remembered what she'd felt like pressed against him, and the effects of the cold shower wore off in an instant.

Merda.

She looked at him. 'You wanted to talk to your assistant?'

He'd forgotten completely. 'Yes.'

'Is it okay if I shower first? And then I'll bring the phone down.'

Dax made some sound of assent and tried not to imagine Laia in the shower.

She padded upstairs to the bedrooms.

Dax wasn't sure what he'd expected, and it should be a *good* thing that she obviously wasn't going to make any reference to the kiss, but it also made him feel prickly.

Had she taken his words to heart and put it down to a mistake, too? Happy to forget about it? Even though he would bet that it had been as erotic an experience for her as it had been for him, if her reaction had been anything to go by.

Now he felt incensed that she seemed inclined to ignore it. Which was ridiculous. He'd betrayed his brother just by kissing her! He'd created a situation where he would have to endure watching Laia by Ari's side while the memory of that kiss burned a hole in his gut.

No. It was just a kiss. A kiss that meant nothing.

Dax cursed again and went to the kitchen, randomly pulling out ingredients. He needed to make himself busy.

After about half an hour, Laia was back.

Dax's brain went blank for a second. She was wearing cut-off shorts and a Lycra crop top that lovingly outlined her breasts. Her waist dipped in and flared out again gently. Her skin was smooth and golden. Dark hair was pulled back into a damp plait.

It took him a moment to realise she was holding out the phone. 'John is on speaker.'

Dax's brain was sluggish. He wanted to snatch the phone from her and instruct his assistant to send a plane, helicopter—*anything*—immediately. But he couldn't. He gritted his jaw and forced himself to focus, then reeled off a list of things he wanted his assistant to work on.

When he was finished, Laia terminated the call. She made a little whistling sound. 'What did your last slave die of?'

Dax forced himself not to respond. 'A lot of people depend on me for their livelihoods.' He winced inwardly. He sounded like his brother now. Uptight. Ha! Ari would laugh his head off.

Laia looked sheepish as she put the phone in a back pocket. 'I'm sorry, I know you have responsibilities.'

Dax went still. 'Not so long ago you were saying the opposite.'

A dark flush came into her cheeks. She looked at his mouth, and then back up. 'I… That wasn't fair. Like you said, I don't know the background.'

She looked at his mouth again. Suddenly all Dax could hear was the rush of blood to his head. He wanted to kiss her again. And this time not stop.

He moved back around the kitchen island. He was determined to pretend it had never happened.

And that's going really well, mocked a little voice.

'I'm making a seafood platter for dinner, okay?'

'Sounds perfect. I'm going down to the pontoon. Some fresh supplies are coming in.'

Dax looked at her. She was backing away.

'Needless to say, please don't try anything. The security guards will be watching.'

Dax was irritated that his first thought wasn't to devise some way to overcome the boatman and make his escape, but to welcome some distance between him and Laia. Right now, if she'd told him she was leaving him on the island while she went back to the mainland he would have welcomed it.

* * *

Laia carried the bags back up to the villa. Her face burned when she thought of one thing in particular that she'd ordered. A big box of condoms.

The box was light in the bag, but it felt like a ton weight. Weighed down by her hubris in thinking that she could entice Dax into more than a kiss. He'd made no reference to it just now. Clearly sending a signal that it had been, as he'd called it, a mistake.

But *he* had kissed *her*. So she knew he wanted her.

Her conscience pricked again at the thought of pitting him against his brother, but as far as she was concerned his brother had no jurisdiction here and no claim over her. This was her last few days as a free woman. And she wanted Dax to be her first lover.

What if it hadn't worked out like this? Would you still be hating Prince Dax or would you be able to move on?

As Laia huffed her way up the steps she had to concede that if she'd never come face to face with Dax again then she might have fooled herself into believing she disapproved of him and didn't find him remotely attractive.

But all it would have taken would have been a face-to-face meeting like this one and she would have been forced to acknowledge her desire and complicated feelings for the man.

In a way, it was a blessing that it was happening now, here on this island. She could put Dax and her attraction to him behind her after this. Move on with no regrets. No unfulfilled fantasies.

First you have to sleep with him, reminded a little voice.

Laia got to the top step, out of breath, sweat running down her forehead and between her breasts.

Suddenly Dax appeared, and Laia had to take a moment to appreciate the incongruity of the image—the world's most infamous playboy with a tea towel thrown over his shoulder.

And yet it didn't diminish his sex appeal one little bit. If anything, the hint of domesticity added to it.

Once again he looked totally at ease and at home in shorts and a polo shirt open at the neck. Laia wanted to press her mouth there and then move it down, over his chest, her teeth finding a nipple, biting gently before—

'Bags?'

Dax interrupted her suddenly rampant imagination and she saw he was holding his hands out to take the bags. Laia handed them over, but at the last second remembered and kept one back, clutching it to her chest muttering, 'Feminine products.'

The thought of Dax seeing the box of condoms was too horrifying to contemplate.

He went back towards the kitchen. 'I'll put these away.'

Laia fled upstairs with her cargo and put the box deep into one of the bathroom cabinets. She looked at herself in the mirror. Eyes wide, cheeks flushed. She looked guilty. She was in full on crush mode and it was heady. She'd never really fancied anyone before.

Because it had always been Dax.

Feeling restless, Laia locked her door and dug out her phone, hoping that there might be a message from Maddi, but there was nothing. She suspected that Maddi had disabled her phone in a bid to protect Laia.

Laia went online to check what was happening, and saw pictures of King Aristedes and Maddi at a posh Santanger restaurant having lunch.

Maddi was wearing a jumpsuit, her arms bare. She looked very sleek and very beautiful. The King was wearing a suit. Laia immediately compared him to Dax. They were similarly good-looking, but where Aristedes was all clean lines and a neat, short beard hugging his jaw, Laia knew that Dax in the same scenario would be somehow...messy. Either his hair, or the stubble on his jaw that he couldn't be bothered to shave after a night of passion with his latest lover...

He'd certainly given that impression every time he'd appeared in the tabloids.

Laia emitted a sound of frustration and got off the bed to pace back and forth. Everything in her education and upbringing had schooled her to find King Aristedes attractive. Not his reprobate brother.

But his brother was the one she wanted with every pulse of her blood.

For the first time in her life she had to recognise that there was wildness in her. A wildness that had been awoken the first time she'd laid eyes on Dax. That had lain dormant until they'd met again.

It was since that night in Monte Carlo that she'd begun avoiding King Aristedes in earnest. As if she'd been reminded of what she wanted even as she'd denied it to herself.

She went back to the laptop and looked at the pictures of Maddi again. Searching for a sign that her sister was somehow in peril or unhappy. If she saw even a hint of it she would arrange for someone to go and get her out of there, but there was no hint of discomfort or unhappiness.

To the contrary. She and the King were conversing intently. Totally engrossed with each other.

A tiny seed of a suspicion formed in Laia's head as she looked at the pictures. Could it be possible that her sister and the King weren't just acting out a fake engagement?

Laia put her hand to her mouth at the notion. She knew Maddi would do anything for her, that her loyalty was true and deep. But Laia had made it very clear that she had no intention of marrying Aristedes, so even if there was something between Maddi and Aristedes, Laia wouldn't consider it a betrayal.

Laia also knew Maddi had a pragmatic approach to emotions and the notion of love. But as for desire…? As Laia was beginning to understand, once desire was involved all bets were off.

Considering her own situation… If Dax was determined to ignore the kiss, how was Laia going to remind him? And, more pertinently, encourage him to do it again?

Dax felt suspicious and he didn't know why. Well, that was a lie. He knew exactly why. Because he suspected Laia was up to something.

Since she'd brought the shopping up from the boat she'd appeared periodically during the course of the rest of the day, in those maddening cut-off shorts and the little crop top.

A tiny bikini was the only item of clothing that would have been more exposing.

First she'd helped him clear up his prep for dinner—
he'd made the most of the fresh seafood the boatman
had delivered and added it to the dish.

Then she'd gone off to do some gardening, reappear-
ing with mud dotted on her knees and arms and face,
carrying a big bunch of wild flowers that she'd artfully
arranged in a huge vase.

Then, while he'd been watching a documentary in
the media room, she'd appeared and asked very genially
if he'd like anything. The sun had been going down, so
he'd asked for a beer.

And now he sat here, nursing his beer and not con-
centrating on the documentary.

Had she really decided that their kiss was a mistake too? She was certainly behaving as if it hadn't
happened.

It shouldn't be bothering him, because it had been
weak and wrong to kiss her, but...

Dax's hand gripped the beer bottle. *Por Dios*, it had
felt like heaven.

He gave up on the documentary and switched off
the TV. He went out into the kitchen area and came to
a standstill.

Laia was naked.

He blinked. She wasn't naked. But she was wearing
a slinky silky slip of a dress that was approximately
one shade lighter than her own skin tone.

She hadn't noticed him standing there in mute shock,
taking her in.

The dress had delicate spaghetti straps that looked
as if they'd slip down a shoulder at any moment. There
was a slightly dipped ruched bit at the front. It belatedly

occurred to Dax that she wasn't wearing a bra, because he could see no straps.

Her hair was up in an unfussy bun and her feet were bare. No jewellery, no adornment. She didn't need it.

She was the image of understated sexiness. And that was before he noticed there was a slit on one side of the dress, so when she moved a length of very toned thigh was revealed.

She saw him and stood up from where she'd been checking something in the oven. She smiled brightly. 'Shall I prepare the last bits for dinner and set the table?'

Dax had never cooked dinner with a woman before. Cooking was something he enjoyed privately. It was far too intimate to share.

'Okay.'

Laia gestured vaguely towards his clothes. 'Don't feel like you have to make an effort just because I did.'

Dax's gaze narrowed on her. His Spidey senses were tingling. 'Laia, what are you up to?'

Her eyes widened. 'What? I felt like dressing up a little. There are never usually guests here.'

'Oh, so now I'm a guest? Call your boatman friend back and have him pick me up in an hour.'

Laia's face paled a little, and for a second Dax thought she actually looked...*hurt*. Which was ridiculous. Except he had a sense at that moment—out of nowhere—of affinity. As if she knew what it was to feel alone, too.

When he and Ari had been separated so that Ari could concentrate on his important studies, Dax had spent long hours playing alone in the palace. In many ways when his mother had sought him out more and more Dax had almost welcomed it, because he'd felt lonely. He just hadn't realised how claustrophobic her attention would become. Or how all-consuming.

Dax noticed Laia was drawing back into herself, smoothing her expression. Becoming the polished Princess again. And he didn't welcome it. He had to admit that if she told him he could leave right now, he'd hesitate. More than hesitate.

And he couldn't pretend that it had anything to do with persuading her to go to his brother and fulfil her obligations.

The woman behind the Princess, who walked around in cut-off shorts and bare feet and little teasing crop tops…who kissed like a siren from a mythical tale… was tying him in knots. And he had a feeling she knew it too.

But he wasn't going to play her game. He had more control than that.

He put down his beer and said, 'I'm joking, of course. Why would I leave this beautiful place and such a generous host? I'll freshen up.'

Laia cursed herself when Dax left the kitchen. She had to stop looking so obviously hurt when he said he wanted to leave. Of course he didn't want to be here— she'd trapped him!

But still… She'd thought that in spite of everything there was…*something* between them. Apart from all the obvious things they had in common, like both being from royal dynasties.

And that kiss.

She made a face at the dress she'd chosen to wear.

She'd pulled it out on a whim. She knew it was audacious. She felt naked in it. But if she was going to test Dax's control then she didn't have much time to lose.

He struck her as a man who prided himself on his control, which she realised ran contrary to what she'd assumed about him before she'd got to know him.

Like a lot of other things that ran contrary to what she'd expected…

A timer went off and Laia broke out of her reverie and turned off the grill. The array of seafood looked mouthwateringly delicious. Grilled lobster, snapper fillet, pepper prawns and calamari. She helped herself to a juicy prawn, using her fingers, and almost groaned at the taste. She could see how food like this was an aphrodisiac.

Before she made a complete fool of herself—or, worse, ate all the food, she set the table with a candle and a small posy of flowers in a vase. She turned the lighting down.

She felt anxious. She'd never tried to seduce a man before.

She heard a sound and turned around—and felt winded. Dax was wearing dark trousers and a white shirt. Open at his throat. Sleeves rolled up. His hair was damp. His jaw was still stubbled. She'd had a slight burn after their kiss earlier.

Her insides clenched tight when she thought of how it had felt when his tongue had touched hers and the kiss had spiralled into a dizzying white-hot fire.

She really, really wanted to kiss him again.

She could feel the tension in the air between them. The push and pull.

She forced her mind to focus. 'The food is ready. I can serve?'

'I'll get the wine.' He looked at her with mock severity. 'Only one glass for you.'

Laia rolled her eyes, relieved at the break in tension.

She brought the platter of seafood and some plates over to the table. At first she tried to be polite, using a knife and fork, but when she saw Dax pick up some lobster with his fingers, she gave up and joined him.

It felt thoroughly decadent, eating with her fingers, and very sensual.

The butter sauce from the lobster ran down her chin, and before she could get it Dax had leaned over and wiped it with his thumb. He looked as surprised as she felt. It had been such an automatically intimate gesture. He wiped his thumb with his napkin, and Laia's insides tightened as she couldn't help but imagine that he'd put it into his mouth instead.

She was losing it.

After that she avoided his eye for a bit. Mortified.

They ate in companionable silence, and after a few minutes Laia put her fork down and wiped her mouth. She took a sip of the crisp white wine, gestured to the half-decimated platter of seafood.

'This is seriously impressive. You could probably get work as a chef if you lost everything tomorrow.'

Dax wiped his own mouth. 'Good to know.'

'My half-sister loves food. She's a good cook too— she's the one who has been teaching me.'

Dax sat back, wine glass stem between his fingers. 'What's she like?'

'Well…' Laia hesitated.

She was wary, considering both how Dax had reacted to learning about her and what was potentially happening right now between her sister and King Aristedes. She didn't know how Dax would feel about that.

But he said, 'Genuine question.'

Laia relaxed marginally. 'She's physically very like me…as you saw. Except her eyes are more hazel. And she's curvier. And she has a gap between her front teeth.' Laia couldn't help smiling. 'She's sweet and open. There's no agenda with Maddi. She's quite shy. She's a little terrified of becoming a princess. The plan is to let people know around the time of the coronation, so that's when she'll be officially acknowledged…'

'Yet she jumped into the frying pan with Ari…? A ballsy move.'

'She's brave.'

'And she isn't resentful that she didn't grow up with great privilege?'

Laia shook her head. 'No—amazingly. But she did admit she missed not knowing our father. She's pretty special. She's much more open and affectionate than me. She's quite unorthodox… Not a hippy, exactly, but she goes with the flow…'

Dax let out a little huff of laughter. 'It sounds like Ari won't know what's hit him.'

Laia shifted uncomfortably, thinking of those pictures again.

Dax said, 'She does sound like a special person. She'd have to be to not grow up with a huge chip on her shoulder after being ostracised from a life of royalty.'

Laia said, 'The ironic thing is that I always wished for a sibling when I was growing up. I was lonely. But, as you've said, you were separated from Aristedes, so even if Maddi had been there, maybe I wouldn't have seen her all that much.' Before she could stop herself, Laia asked, 'Do you see yourself having children?'

She noticed that Dax kept his expression carefully schooled before answering.

'Like marriage, it's not something I've ever envisaged. After my experience with my parents, who didn't really parent at all, I can't say it's something I'd want to risk inflicting on my children.'

'But Aristedes has no choice.'

'Just like you have no choice.'

'I had a good experience with my father. He was loving and kind and supportive. But not having had a mother... I think I'm afraid that I won't know what to do. How to mother.'

Laia was shocked. She'd never admitted that out loud to anyone. Not even Maddi.

Dax said, 'I don't know much about these things, but for what it's worth I don't doubt that it's an entirely instinctive process and you'd be a great mother.'

Laia blinked. Startled at the sudden welling of moisture in her eyes. She'd never in a million years have imagined this conversation with this man. She'd never expected to feel such emotion.

Her voice was husky. 'I... Thank you. You didn't have to say that.'

'I don't say things I don't mean.'

No, he didn't. Just as he didn't lead women on.

He would be a good father. Laia felt it in her bones. She could almost see him with a small, sturdy toddler with dark hair, lifting him high in the air.

She stood up quickly, before any more disturbing images could pop into her head or she blurted out something else incredibly exposing. She couldn't even blame the wine this time. She'd had hardly any.

She gathered up the plates and said brightly, 'Coffee?'

'I think I'll have a digestif…a little whisky.'

Dax got up and helped clear the table, before going over to the drinks cabinet and pouring himself a measure of whisky.

Laia made coffee and went out to the deck to see if some air might help her regain some composure. There was a full moon casting a milky glow over the dark forest and the sea beyond. The lights of the fishermen shone in the distance.

She sensed Dax coming to stand near her. After that conversation Laia felt as if her skin had been peeled back to reveal a tender under-layer. She felt even more acutely aware of him, felt her blood humming under sensitive skin.

The intense heat of the day was gone, and in its place was the night-time cloak of tropical warmth. Laia turned around and rested back against the wooden railing. She looked at Dax and her heart tripped.

She said, 'You aren't at all what I expected.'

He turned towards her and hitched a hip onto the thick wood. 'What did you expect?'

'A petulant spoiled playboy with the attention span of a gnat.'

Dax made a face. 'A little unfair.'

Laia was indignant. 'You've admitted that you cultivated that reputation.'

He had the grace to look a little sheepish.

'Except now I get the impression that you're at a fork in the road,' she went on. 'You can't keep up the playboy façade…you've already started to retire it. People are wondering what's going on. What's next for Prince Dax?'

Laia could see that he didn't like being questioned.

He took a sip of whisky. Looked at her. 'Maybe I'm ready to out myself as a serious businessman?'

But not a husband and father.

Before she could quiz him any more he said, 'I've been meaning to ask you…what was going on with you that night in the club in Monte Carlo? You were on your own, lost to the world…you'd obviously stayed up past your bedtime.'

Laia felt a little jolt. The fact that he'd noticed her in that moment made her feel a little emotional.

She gave a little shrug. 'I guess I wanted to not be me for a moment. To pretend that I was someone else. Someone without duty and obligations and every second of my life mapped out. Right down to the man I'm supposed to marry, whether I like it or not. I was fantasising that I was just a normal girl…out for the night with endless possibilities in front of me. And then I opened my eyes and there you were.'

'You didn't know who I was at first.'

Laia hated it that he'd noticed that. Noticed her little moment of exposure. 'But then I did.'

'And you realised I was the Big Bad Wolf so you ran.'

Laia looked at Dax. The man in front of her was the same man who'd been in front of her that night, but this time everything was different.

Very carefully she said, 'I don't want to run now.'

* * *

'What did you say?'

But Dax had heard Laia perfectly well, and his body had heard her too. Every muscle was tense with need. His pulse was racing and his blood was hot.

She was looking at him very directly. 'I said, I don't want to run now.'

Dax knew he should be cutting this off, walking away, but a devil inside him made him say, 'Why don't you want to run?'

Her cheeks went pink, and in the midst of this heightening tension between them Dax had the urge to reach out and run his knuckles down her cheeks. He clenched his hand by his side. His other hand was tight around the glass.

He wasn't sure how he'd managed to eat and converse like a normal person over dinner, when all he'd been aware of was that slip of a dress and how it draped forward to expose the upper slopes of Laia's breasts every time she moved.

She's doing this on purpose.

Dax tried to exert some control over his body. His head.

But then she stood up straight, faced him directly, and said, 'I don't want to run because I want you.'

Dax's attempts to exert control dissolved in a flood of heat. He gritted his jaw. 'I can't deny that I want you too, Laia, but it's not happening. That kiss was a mistake.'

'It didn't feel like a mistake.'

Dax moved back into the kitchen, put his glass down on the counter.

Laia followed him and put her cup down.

No, it hadn't felt like a mistake…it had felt sweet and sinful all at once.

'You are marrying my brother.'

Laia waved a hand. 'Look around you. We're thousands of miles from Santanger. Does it look like I'm marrying your brother?'

Dax clenched his jaw again. Against the temptation she posed. He had to admit that up until the kiss he'd held out some thread of hope or futile belief that she would somehow come to her senses and return to Europe.

He shook his head, as if that would rearrange his brain cells into forgetting he wanted this woman. 'I came here to track you down for my brother. I won't betray him.'

He could see that she looked frustrated. She said tautly, 'Your brother and I have no relationship to betray.'

Laia's hair had started to come undone and was falling in tendrils around her face. Her eyes were so green they reminded him of the sea around the island. Her jaw was tight. He could feel the tension in her body, as if connected to her by an invisible thread.

So far, all his little acts of rebellion had never impacted Ari. Dax had made sure of that. He'd always stayed within the bounds of acceptability.

Laia was not the rock he would perish on. She was just a woman he wanted. She was not unique.

So why does it feel like you've never wanted another woman? How is that you can't even picture your last lover?

Like earlier, Dax knew he needed to put distance between them. *Now.*

He said, 'I'm not having this conversation. There's nothing to discuss.'

He turned and went towards the stairs leading up to his suite, where he intended on taking a very cold shower for a very long time. Maybe he could freeze this desire out of his body. In spite of the tropical temperatures.

He had his foot on the bottom step when Laia said from behind him, 'It's your fault, you know. It's your fault I can't marry your brother.'

CHAPTER SEVEN

LAIA'S HEART WAS thumping so hard she felt light-headed. Dax had gone very still. Slowly, he turned around. His expression was suspiciously blank.

He came back towards her. He stopped a couple of feet away. Laia could feel the tension like electricity crackling between them.

He gritted out one word. 'Explain.'

Laia swallowed. Dax suddenly seemed a foot taller. Broader. Darker. She hadn't fully thought through what his reaction might be. Explosive, she was guessing.

'Laia?'

How did she even articulate this? It suddenly seemed ridiculous that he could have had such a huge impact on her since—

'You do not get to make a claim like that and then say nothing.'

Dax had folded his arms, which only drew attention to his muscles, pushing against the thin material of his shirt.

'How is it my fault, exactly? And why am I the only one still talking?'

She spoke. 'The first time we met…in Paris… You…

affected me. I fancied you. I developed a crush on you. A big one. You were the most beautiful man I'd ever seen. And then you told me you were going to be my brother-in-law one day and I felt sick at the thought— because how could I feel such illicit things for my brother?'

Dax's face lost some of its ferocity. 'You were only sixteen.'

Laia shrugged. 'Old enough to form a crush. And then when I saw what you were doing…how you were living your life…all the women… I think I was jealous. But I told myself you disgusted me, because you were so flagrantly disregarding the fact that you were a crown prince and had responsibilities to your King and your people. I felt ashamed that you were attractive to me when I was trying my best to prove to everyone that I could be Queen some day. But that night in Monte Carlo… I couldn't hide my immediate response to you. I envied your freedom. And then I was angry because I was weak enough to be jealous… The truth is that I convinced myself I disapproved of you to deny admitting how much you affected me. On some very deep fundamental level I knew I couldn't marry King Aristedes because I wanted you. Not him.'

Dax's voice was a little hoarse. 'You haven't even given him a chance…'

Laia shook her head. 'I saw him after my father's funeral. I felt nothing for him. *Nothing*. And he dismissed me. He's not interested in me at all. On any level. And that's not good enough. I've measured every man I've met against you, without even realising what I was doing. That's why…it's your fault.'

Dax took a step closer. His eyes were piercing her all the way down to where Laia had nothing left to hide. She'd exposed herself spectacularly. There was no going back.

Dax said, 'Ari is a good man. He would respect you and treat you well. You would want for nothing.'

'Except passion.'

Now Dax's cheeks flushed. 'You want a lot from your marriage. Passion *and* love?'

Laia felt defensive. 'I don't think that's too much to ask. After I leave here, my life will not be my own ever again. Not really. Is it so selfish to want something for myself while I can still have it? When I'm hidden from the world and no one will ever be any the wiser?'

Dax's jaw clenched. 'And then you can get on with your life and find this true love? This paragon of a mate who will fulfil all your needs? Why don't you just wait for him?'

'Because I don't think I'll be able to move on until—' She stopped.

'Until?' Dax prompted.

'Until I've *known* you.'

'You mean until we've had sex?' Dax said crudely.

Laia winced. 'Not like that.'

Except it was exactly like that.

For the first time Laia felt vulnerable. She doubted herself. Maybe she wasn't a match for Dax's control after all.

'I truly didn't know this would happen. That you would be here like this. But now the thought of meeting you at some future event or place and realising

how much I want you, not having known you, it ter-
rifies me…'

'Laia, Ari is—'

She cut him off. 'Not the man I want. Ever. I will
never be with him. That's what I realised on a very
deep level all those years ago. I can't be with him when
I want you.'

Dax seemed to struggle with something for a long
second, and then he said, with almost palpable reluctance, 'The truth is that you've haunted me since I saw
you in Monaco. And until I saw you again I've had no
interest in much at all.'

Laia had to lock her knees to stay standing. Her legs
were turning to jelly. Was she part of the reason he'd
disappeared from the scene?

Feeling emboldened, she took a step closer to Dax.
She could feel his heat. And his scent, a potent mix of
wood and musk and something uniquely him, tickled
her nostrils.

She said, 'Let me put it this way. If I told you to send
me to your brother right now, to become his Queen,
would you be happy to let me go to him?'

Laia took a deep breath and made the biggest gam-
ble of her life.

'Because if you say yes, then I'll go. Leave now. Not
to go to him, but I'll go home and let the chips fall where
they may. I'll never see you again.' She lifted her chin.
'I have some pride, Dax. I won't beg.'

Dax closed the distance between them. There was
barely an inch now. He was all she could see.

Laia bit her lip. If he said *Yes, go now* she might very
well die a little inside.

But he didn't say anything for a long moment, and then he lifted his hand and tugged her lower lip free from her teeth. Laia held her breath. Dax's gaze was on her mouth.

He said, almost to himself, 'Would I be happy to let you go to him…?'

He shook his head, and then he looked at her and she could see fires blazing in his eyes. A slow surge of euphoria made its way into her blood.

'No, Laia, I wouldn't be happy to let you go to him, or to anyone else. Because I want you and I'm done fighting it. You're mine.'

Laia trembled. She'd campaigned for this—she'd asked for it…all but begged for it. But was she really ready for it?

A kaleidoscope of pictures flashed through her head: seeing him that first time in Paris, all the tabloid images she'd pored over for years, Monte Carlo and now here. This moment. This man.

Yes.

She put her hand on his chest, over his heart, and said, 'Then make me yours, Dax.'

Dax had tipped over the edge of any control he possessed and was walking through fire. Let this woman go? Walk away? Without tasting her?

The thought made him feral.

He finally understood that Laia absolutely meant what she said. She had no intention of ever marrying his brother. In truth, he'd understood it for a while, but he'd been fighting his own desire because he'd never, ever gone against Ari in his life.

But something Laia had said had resonated with him. She selfishly wanted to take something for herself. While the eyes of the world were turned away.

In doing this, Dax would be embarking on the most selfish thing he'd ever done. And in many ways the worst thing he'd ever done. Taking his brother's promised bride.

If he'd felt tainted and damned by the past before, now he would be tainted and damned in the present. But there was no turning back. He knew Ari had no real appreciation for this woman. He'd always known it. Laia was right—Ari just saw her as the next step.

Even so, Dax knew he was crossing a line and he would never forgive himself. He would have to add this to the line he'd crossed that day of the car crash. He was good at crossing lines and accepting guilt. He'd accepted that a long time ago.

And there was no way he could hold back from what this woman was offering. She was sweet and pure and light—and, fatally, he was drawn to her as if she could offer him some kind of absolution. He did not deserve this. But he was taking it.

There was no other choice—there never had been. He could see that now—he was filled with a primal need to possess that he'd never experienced before.

He put his hand over Laia's on his chest. The way she did that...it pierced something inside him, some of the darkness. He threaded his fingers through hers and then, taking her hand, he led her through the villa and up the stairs.

The night was warm and soft around them. Only

the night chorus of insects and small animals broke the peace.

But Dax couldn't even hear that. All he could hear was the pounding of his blood. And his heart.

Laia felt as if she was in some kind of dreamlike state as she followed Dax up the stairs, her hand in his, fingers entwined, as if they'd been lovers for years.

There was no hesitation.

The lights were low, infusing everything with a low golden glow, and Dax led her into his bedroom and closed the door. He let her hand go and went over to the shutters, pulling them closed. Then he dropped the net around the bed.

Laia watched him. He turned around and came towards her. He stopped in front of her.

'Turn around.'

Laia did as he said. He pulled her hair free, so that it fell down her back. He put his hands on her shoulders and turned her again to face him. Her skin felt so sensitive.

But he didn't touch her straight away. He said, 'I've suspected something, but I need to know…'

Laia knew what he was going to say, and she knew it would be futile to pretend otherwise. So she swallowed her self-consciousness and said, 'I'm not experienced. At all.'

A muscle pulsed in Dax's jaw. 'No lovers?'

She shook her head.

'Laia…are you sure you don't want to do this with the man who will be your husband?'

She shook her head.

'I'm not naive enough to confuse sex with love.' She made a face. 'If my father's affair has taught me anything it's that. This…this thing that's between us. You said it's rare. I might never feel this again, even with the man I choose to marry. I know that.' Just so he was in no doubt, she said, 'I choose you to be my first lover, Dax. But don't worry, I won't fall in love with you.'

His mouth twisted. 'No. Because I'm not really a suitable consort for a queen, am I?'

His words sank in and suddenly it felt as if the earth was tilting sideways. She put out her hands to find balance, but Dax was already holding her steady, his hands on her arms.

He was frowning. 'Okay?'

Laia nodded. 'Just a little rush of blood…'

But she knew something had just happened. Something profound that she couldn't—or didn't want to—analyse just yet. A desire for him to be hers in spite of all the reasons why he couldn't—because he had no intention of settling down.

Desperate to avoid thinking about that, Laia said, 'Kiss me, Dax.'

He brought one hand up, over her arm and shoulder, under her hair, and cupped her neck, tugging her closer. 'Now, that I can do.'

He seemed to take for ever to touch his mouth to hers. Laia had the slightest glimpse of his wicked smile and she was about to scowl or beg. But then everything was forgiven, because his mouth was on hers and Laia's entire body was suffused with heat and electric excitement.

She'd thought she'd made too much of their kiss earlier…that it couldn't possibly have been that transformative…but it was happening again. And it was even more profound, because now she was even hungrier for it. Desperate.

She hadn't even realised she'd twined her arms around Dax's neck, arching her body against his, wanting to feel that whipcord strength against her body, hard against soft.

She'd never considered herself a very girly girl, but she'd never felt more feminine than she did in this moment. Never been so aware of the differences between a man and a woman.

Dax's other hand was splayed across her back, and she could feel him moving it up now, over her bare skin, finding one of the straps of her dress and slipping his fingers underneath to dislodge it.

But then he tensed and stopped. Pulled back.

Laia opened her eyes. Her mouth already felt swollen. Breath fast and choppy. 'What is it?'

Dax's face was flushed, eyes glittering. 'I don't have anything with me…' He cursed softly and let her go.

Laia struggled to make her sluggish brain work. 'You don't have what with you?'

He put his hands on his hips. 'Protection. I don't have protection. We can't do this. I'm not risking getting you pregnant. That's a scandal too far even for me.'

Finally what he'd said sank in, and with it came a wave of relief.

She said, 'Wait there.' And fled back across the hall to her room, fingers clumsy with the key to the door. Eventually it opened and she almost fell inside. She went straight to where she'd stashed the box of condoms and picked it up.

She brought it back to Dax and handed it to him.

He took it and looked at it. And then her. He said, 'The delivery earlier today?'

Laia nodded, feeling self-conscious. 'I only thought of it when…after the kiss… Obviously I can't risk getting pregnant…'

Dax shook his head faintly. 'Not many women have ever surprised me… No, scratch that—actually no woman has ever surprised me as much as you have.'

Laia said, 'Is it…are there enough?'

Dax looked at the box and huffed out a laugh. He opened it and took out one foil-wrapped sheath.

'Let's start with one and see how we go, okay?'

Laia had never felt so gauche or out of her depth.

Dax seemed to take pity on her. He put down the protection and led her over to the bed.

He stood in front of her. 'Laia, I don't want you to regret this. You're about to become Queen. Life for you and my brother is different. When you meet the man you'll marry he'll probably expect you to be—'

'Pure?' Laia cut Dax off. 'I've done my best to get out of one medieval marriage arrangement. I'm not going to keep myself pure, like some sort of sacrificial offering for my husband. I'm a modern woman, Dax, and the only reason I'm still a virgin is because I've never had the opportunity to lose my virginity. Most men are too scared to come near me—they're put off by the fact that I'm promised already—and if it isn't that they're just intimidated by my status. Apart from all that, I have practically no privacy. I'm watched over day and night.

Here…with you… This is the first time in a long time that I've been truly on my own. And it's not just that you happen to be here and it's an opportunity. *You're* the man I want. The man I've wanted for so long. The fact that you're here is…serendipitous. It's like a gift… *you're* a gift.'

Everything in Dax rejected her assertion that he was a gift, while at the same he was inordinately moved by her words.

Dax wasn't anyone's gift. He brought with him a legacy of guilt and tragedy. A debauched reputation. And yet here, now, in front of Laia, who was looking at him with such pure desire, he felt ridiculously that he was being reborn on some level.

He reached out and touched her jaw. So delicate, yet strong. Like her. He felt humble all of a sudden. This woman was a queen—maybe not quite yet, but she would be, very soon. And he could imagine her being a great queen. Strong and proud, but also soft and compassionate.

Ari had been a fool not to take more care to make her feel wanted. She would have been a great Queen of Santanger. But she wasn't Ari's, and in that moment Dax felt a surge of emotion as he fully acknowledged that she wanted him.

'I don't deserve you…*this*.'

Laia shook her head. 'Why would you say such a thing? Of course you deserve me. I'm really not that—'

Dax put his finger on her mouth, stopping her words. 'Don't you dare say it. You are a woman descended from great women, who have endured all manner of things to be Queen of their land. And you are about to become Queen. You're already a queen.'

He saw Laia's throat work as she swallowed. And then she took a step closer to him and put her hand on his wrist, pulling his hand away from her mouth.

'Can we just…stop talking? And make love?'

Dax couldn't help huffing out a laugh. No woman had ever accused him of talking too much. But of course with this woman everything was reversed and upside down.

'Yes, we can.'

He took a step back. He wanted nothing more than to rip that excuse of a dress from her body and sink so deep inside her that all the things she made him feel and all the contradictions would be eclipsed.

But now was not the time. He would have to go slowly, even if it killed him.

'Undress me, Laia.'

She looked up at him, her lip caught between her teeth. Dax curled his hands into fists to stop himself from touching her. She brought her hands to his shirt and started to undo his buttons. He saw how she concentrated. He also saw the almost discernible tremor in her hands. She was nervous. He'd never had to worry about that before, because his lovers had always been experienced.

He let her undo all the buttons on his shirt. She pulled it out of his trousers. Then her hands went to his belt buckle and his every nerve-ending was tingling. She opened the belt. Then the top button of his trousers. The zip.

Dax held his breath. He could hear Laia's breath

coming faster. The dress dipped down between her breasts and he caught tantalising glimpses of soft, plump swells. Her nipples were hard. He imagined the silk material of the dress brushing against them. Sensitising them even more.

Unable to hold back, Dax reached out and cupped Laia's breast through her dress. She sucked in a breath and looked up. He kept his eyes on her and took his hand from her breast to pull down the other strap of her dress. She lifted her arms free. The dress gaped and Dax tugged it ever so slightly, until it dropped all the way down, exposing one breast.

'You are…beautiful,' he breathed in awe.

Her skin was luminous, dark golden. Her breast was perfectly shaped. Pert and plump. Succulent. The nipple was hard, pouting forward from the areola. Dax cupped her flesh and rubbed his thumb back and forth over the hard, straining nipple.

Laia was very still. Hardly breathing now. He looked up. Her eyes were unfocused.

He reached for the other strap and pulled it down, exposing her other breast. The dress clung to her hips.

Dax finished taking off his clothes until he was naked before her. He felt something reverent move through him, as if he was offering himself to her for her delectation.

Her eyes moved over him, shy at first, and then avid. Over his chest and waist and then down. Colour suffused her cheeks as she took him in. Took in how much he wanted her. How hard he was for her.

He ached.

Her eyes were wide. He could see in them something

that looked like trepidation. He took her hand and put it on his chest, over his heart. She looked up.

'Don't think about it. Just let it…happen.'

He led her over to the bed, pulling back the net curtain. She climbed onto the bed.

'Lie back,' Dax instructed.'

She did. Her hair swung around her head in a dark silken tangle. Dax reached forward and tugged the dress down over her hips and off. Now she just wore her underwear. Lacy and flesh-coloured. Provocative. For a moment he almost imagined she was actually experienced, silently laughing at him taking so much care of her.

When had he become so infected by cynicism?

He came down alongside her and spread his hand on her belly. He felt her muscles contracting.

She put her hand on his. 'Dax, you don't have to treat me like spun glass. I won't break.'

If she had any sense of how much he wanted her and how much it was costing him to contain it she might not be so eager. But Dax let his hand drift up to cover her breast, cupping its weight, teasing first one and then the other, before bringing his mouth to one pebbled nipple and pulling it into his mouth.

He almost lost his life there and then, at the first taste of her flesh. The first feel of that hard nub in his mouth.

Her hands were in his hair and he could feel her moving her hips impatiently. He kept his mouth on her breasts, one and then the other, teasing and tasting mercilessly, as he brought his hand back down over her belly to the top of her underwear.

Sliding his fingers under the front, he felt springy

curls. She opened her legs and Dax lifted his head. He looked at her face as his hand delved deeper, between her legs, his fingers finding the hot, wet centre of her body.

His erection twitched in reaction as his brain registered how she felt. She was biting her lip again, eyes huge. On him. He explored her body, moving his fingers in and out, the slickness of her body sending Dax perilously close to spilling without even entering her.

He covered her mouth with his as his movements became faster, harder, mimicking what would come when she was ready. When he had prepared her.

She was making little moaning sounds. Her back started arching off the bed. Dax urged her on, breathing into her mouth, 'It's okay…let it go, Laia…let it out.'

She did. With a big, keening cry as her body convulsed around his fingers and the waves of her pleasure spread outwards.

Dax had to tense every muscle in his body not to come right then. He let Laia absorb what had happened. And after a minute she opened her eyes again. She was perspiring slightly, and it made her glow. The scent of her arousal was in the air and Dax had never smelled anything sexier or more potent. If he didn't sink inside this woman soon, he might just die.

'Okay?'

She looked at him. Dazed. She nodded. And then she looked embarrassed. 'I've… You know… Before… myself…'

Dax nearly groaned out loud at the thought of her exploring herself. Making herself come.

She continued, her voice slightly hoarse, 'But it never felt like that.'

Dax kissed her slowly, thoroughly. Tongues tangling. He put one of his thighs between her legs and moved his hands over her, exploring every dip and swell and inch of her silken body. She was lithe and firm and soft all at once. He felt as if he'd never really touched a woman before.

When Laia was breathless again, Dax couldn't wait any more.

He pulled back. 'Are you ready?'

Laia nodded. But he could see her trepidation. He said, 'It might sting…hurt a bit at first…but it'll pass, I promise.'

'I trust you.'

For a second Dax couldn't breathe. And then he pushed the emotion out. No room for emotion here.

He encouraged her to lift up, so that he could pull off her underwear. And then he put himself between Laia's legs. Smoothed a hand up one thigh.

He wanted to taste her. Wanted to taste where she'd fallen apart in his hands. But he was too desperate.

He reached for the protection, sending up silent thanks that she'd had the sense to think of it. She was royalty. Soon to be a Queen. The stakes were too high for her to be careless. If she got pregnant by the wrong person—

Dax shut his mind down, because that thought precipitated others, of Laia getting pregnant with the *right* person. And that was not what he wanted to think about right now, when she was spread on the bed for him like his most wicked fantasy…

Dax rolled the protection onto his erection and winced at how sensitive he was. He couldn't remember a time when he'd felt such anticipation to join with a woman.

Laia's breasts were rising and falling rapidly. He could sense her nervousness. He came down and put an arm under her, covered her mouth with his in a deep, drugging kiss. At the same moment he guided himself into the centre of her body—and died a little death at the sensation.

Laia gasped into his mouth as he entered her.

He pulled back. He could feel the sweat on his brow. 'Okay?'

He watched her taking in the sensation. He moved and she winced minutely. Dax immediately wanted to pull out, and started to, but she put a hand on his buttock.

'No, keep going,' she said. 'I'm okay.'

He could see she wasn't, but he did what she asked and thrust deeper. He let her body adjust to his. Tense muscles softening. Accepting his invasion.

Gradually her face lost its slightly pinched look. A kind of curiosity seemed to take her over and she said, a little breathlessly, 'It's okay…really.'

Dax started to move in and out slowly, with excruciating care. His passage became easier, and he could see when discomfort turned to pleasure. A look of wonder came over Laia's face. Wonder and excitement.

She moved under him experimentally, and Dax had to call on every atom of control not to lose it there and then.

She said, 'Dax…you feel…amazing.'

Knowing that she was not in pain gave Dax permission to go a little harder, deeper. He saw the way Laia's eyes were glued to him, as if she was trying to communicate something she didn't understand, and he could feel it in her body as she put her legs around his hips, instinctively chasing the same pinnacle of pleasure that he was hurtling towards.

Silently asking for forgiveness, because he was using his experience and knowledge to send her over the edge before him, Dax reached between them and touched her where their bodies joined. Laia's body tensed around his for an infinitesimal moment before the onslaught of her powerful orgasm finally sent him into oblivion and a pleasure so profound that he just *knew* it was wrong.

Because he didn't deserve anything this pure or pleasurable. Not in a million years.

CHAPTER EIGHT

WHEN LAIA WOKE she heard the call of birds outside. She was alone in her bed. And why shouldn't she be? Something was off though…the sheets were rumpled. And her body felt different, well used. Aching, but in a way that felt…

Laia sat up in bed, completely naked. Something was off because she wasn't in her own bed. Memories flooded through the temporary barrier of sleep.

Last night.

Dax. His big powerful body over hers.

In hers.

The sting of pain and then—a wave of heat washed through her body from her core—then the most incredible, unbelievable pleasure.

She'd fallen asleep with little tingles and tremors under her skin and had woken up at some point to find herself enveloped in Dax's embrace, her back against his front, her bottom snug against his groin. She'd fallen back to sleep wondering if she was dreaming.

Maybe it had been a dream, because she certainly wasn't in Dax's embrace any longer.

She reached for the sheet and pulled it up, even

though she was alone. Where was Dax? What time was it? There was a faint glow of daylight from beyond the net, but not enough for it to be late, yet.

She saw a robe on the end of the bed and was touched by Dax's thoughtfulness. She hadn't expected him to be such a considerate lover.

She pulled on the robe and went to the edge of the bed and pulled back the net. It was early dawn outside, the sky a pinky grey. But she hardly noticed that, because her eye was drawn immediately to the man standing at the wooden railing that ran around the perimeter of the large deck area outside the bedroom.

His back was bare. He wore sweatpants low on his hips. His hair was messy and overlong. She was suddenly blindingly jealous of all the other women who'd seen him like this. Who'd had him in their beds.

She noticed the tension that came into his body when he heard her and a part of her didn't welcome it. He turned his head as she came to stand beside him. She belted the robe tightly around her waist.

'How are you feeling?' he asked.

Laia avoided looking at him for a moment. How did she feel? She realised that she felt powerful. In a very feminine way. As if losing her innocence had fully initiated her into womanhood. Which it had, obviously, but she'd never realised it would feel so profoundly... *significant*.

She'd always seen it as a kind of burden to be got rid of, but what had happened last night with Dax had made her feel humbled. And she realised now she was very grateful that he had been her first lover. Because it had not felt like shedding a burden, it had felt al-most…spiritual.

She would have this knowledge of how it could be inside her for ever.

What if you never experience this again?

Laia went a little cold. She assured herself that she'd seduced him for this very reason—because she'd known it would be like this and this was all she wanted. It wasn't meant to be anything more.

What happens on the island stays on the island.

She couldn't shake a sudden pervasive feeling of in-tense melancholy.

'Laia, are you okay?'

She realised that Dax was still waiting for her an-swer. She took a breath and looked at him, but he im-pacted on her like a punch to the gut, stealing her breath again.

She nodded. 'Fine.'

Amazing.

'Are you sore?'

She shook her head, and blushed as she said, 'A lit-tle, but it's…nice.'

He turned to her fully and reached out to trace a fin-ger along her jaw. There was something in his eyes that made her insides swoop.

'*Nice*…hmm? Was it what you expected?'

No. Because, even though she'd known the facts, Laia had had no idea the experience would be so trans-formative or cataclysmic. But she wasn't going to reveal that to this man who now knew her more intimately than anyone else.

'I guess…'

What she really wanted to say was *thank you*, because she had immense gratitude for what he'd given her: the knowledge of her own sensuality and desirability.

Something flashed in his eyes. 'You *guess*?'

He reached for her, putting a hand around the belt of her robe, and tugged her towards him. She came, with a little stumble, and he caught her against him. She could feel the heat of the day, sultry and humid, rising with the sun.

Dax tipped her chin up so she couldn't escape him. 'Let's see if we can improve on that verdict, hmm?'

Laia trembled with anticipation and not a little apprehension. She didn't know if she could physically survive such an onslaught on her senses—on her body—again, but then she told herself it had been her first time. Surely that was why it had been so intense? And the second time would be...*less*...

But then Dax was kissing her, and stopping her thoughts, and undoing her robe, pushing it off her shoulders and baring her naked body to the warm, tropical dawn.

And then he was leading her back to the bed, and Laia discovered far too late that the second time brought even more intensity. Not less.

When Dax woke after making love to Laia for the second time, the sun was high outside and he could feel the heat. He was in a naked sprawl on the bed, over the covers. *Alone.*

His body felt heavy, with aching muscles and a bone-deep satisfaction that had eluded him for years. The last time he could remember feeling like this had been in the heady days of his first sexual experiences. Before he'd become jaded.

He was glad he was alone, to try and wrap his head around last night and this morning. He'd known the chemistry between him and Laia was off the charts, but in his experience chemistry didn't always translate into the bedroom.

It was because she was a virgin.

Uneasily, Dax didn't think he could put it down to that. It was Laia, uniquely. With her intoxicating mix of reticence and self-consciousness and that innate confidence that came from being purely who she was.

She was a queen. She couldn't help but be regal even in the midst of learning a new experience.

The dominant thing Dax felt right now was humbled. All over again. Because she'd wanted him. Wanted him enough to be her first lover. Even though she wanted to marry for love.

She was such a contradiction. Idealistic and pragmatic at the same time.

Feeling a little exposed—literally—Dax got up and pulled aside the net. The sun was streaming in. He winced. He went into the bathroom and took a shower, and then threw on shorts and a polo shirt. Left his feet bare.

He could get used to this living outside of time feeling. Days melting into nights and back into days. And now, adding Laia in his bed to the mix…? Maybe he'd just lose himself altogether and never re-join the real world? He could understand now why people dropped out of life and went backpacking for years.

Dax heard her low voice as he passed her bedroom and stopped in his tracks, suddenly feeling a little cold. What had he expected? That she'd be downstairs making them a cosy morning-after breakfast? He'd never have encouraged that of a woman in normal circumstances.

But then this woman hadn't conformed to anything *normal* since he'd laid eyes on her in that club. And now, listening to her voice on the other side of the door, he realised that clearly Laia hadn't checked out of the real world. She hadn't lost herself.

Dax put his ear to the door but couldn't make out what she was saying. It sounded like an online meeting. With her advisors? About her coronation? About plans to get on with her life when she went back to Europe?

Quietly, Dax tested the door, but it was locked. He went colder. Last night obviously hadn't blurred the boundaries of what was happening here for her.

He had a very unwelcome feeling of something almost like *hurt*. Laia was just using him to experience what passion felt like before she moved on with her husband of choice. She'd told him as much. Dax was still a prisoner in paradise, and he'd be an idiot to forget it.

Laia terminated the online meeting. She wondered if Giorgio, her advisor, had noticed her dishevelment. She hadn't showered yet. She'd only come into her room earlier because she'd heard her phone ringing in the locked cupboard.

It had been an unwelcome reminder of the outside world after a night and morning of passion such as she never could have imagined. When she'd seen numerous missed calls on her phone she'd gone hot and cold as the pressure of her responsibilities had come back. She'd pulled on a clean top and at the last second had closed and locked her door before joining the meeting.

Giorgio had confirmed that Maddi was still in Santanger and masquerading as Laia, apparently fooling everyone. He'd shown her a picture of them at a charity event and a headline: *The look of love between King Aristedes and his future Queen!*

Laia had studied the picture and had to concede that Maddi didn't look as if she was pretending.

What was going on?

At that moment Laia had heard a sound, like the door handle being turned, but when she'd looked up she'd seen nothing.

She couldn't shake the feeling of guilt at having shut Dax out. They had gone long past the point of locking doors, so she didn't even know why she'd done it. Even if he contacted Aristedes now it was only days to her birthday and the coronation. He wouldn't be able to do anything to stop her being crowned. And sleeping with Dax had as good as put a million nails in the coffin of the marriage agreement.

The real world was encroaching relentlessly, sooner than she liked.

Giorgio had just outlined the arrangements for her return to Isla'Rosa, as soon as she gave the word. But she hadn't been able to give the word. Not yet. Even though she had no real reason to stay here any longer and a million reasons to return home—not least of which was to extricate Maddi from Santanger and figure out what was going on...

But now the meeting was finished, and in spite of Giorgio's urging for her to come home soon, Laia was filled with sense of rebelliousness. Surely another day… another night…couldn't hurt? Surely it wasn't too much to ask when soon she would be handing herself over to a life of duty?

She'd have the rest of her life to think about more serious things. Like becoming Queen. And who she would marry.

When she thought of that, though, she felt cold inside. All she could see was Dax's face above hers, intense and serious as he joined their bodies and transported her to another realm.

When she'd woken again that morning she'd been draped over Dax's naked body. She'd managed to leave without disturbing him and she'd looked back at the last moment, seeing him in that same louche, sexy sprawl that she'd seen him in before.

For a second she'd felt breathless, wondering if it had all been a particularly lurid fantasy. But no. She was naked and aching. And she'd held her scrap of a silk dress in her hand. The dress he had removed from her body.

Laia took a shower. A part of her lamented washing the scent of Dax from her body. The scent of her becoming a woman. She left her hair damp and went into the dressing room. She spotted a white bikini—something she'd never have worn ordinarily, because it was too revealing. But now she imagined wearing it under Dax's gaze, and she was filled with a newfound sense of daring. Or was it confidence?

She pulled on a loose thigh-high kaftan over the bikini and left her room. This time she didn't lock the door. And she hadn't locked away her devices.

She came down into the kitchen area but there was no sign of Dax. She spied the leftovers of a breakfast he'd obviously cooked for himself. She felt a pang of insecurity, disappointment, but then reminded herself that men like Dax didn't *do* cosy mornings-after.

All was quiet. Too quiet.

She felt uneasy, imagining that he'd somehow managed to escape. Maybe he'd had enough and had just left. Vanished back into his life.

The thought was wrenching enough to make Laia pause for a second and consider if she really knew what she was doing. Dancing with the devil.

Except he wasn't a devil. Far from it.

Dax had exploded every misconception she'd had about him. Every judgement.

He was not the man she'd thought he was. Not remotely. She had to acknowledge that she would never have even contemplated making love with him if she'd had any reservations, or if he'd shown a smidgeon of the reputation that followed him.

She knew she wouldn't have slept with him unless she trusted him. And she did. Implicitly. She trusted him with her life.

Laia sat down heavily on a chair, her legs suddenly weak. At what point had she fallen in trust with him? She felt dizzy. She didn't want to have feelings for Dax. He wasn't the man she wanted to care about. Their lives weren't aligned. They wanted different things.

Nothing had changed. She didn't want him for anything beyond the physical. All that was between them was here and now. The present moment. For another day at the most. Twenty-four hours.

She was just feeling something for him because they'd been intimate, and she wasn't experienced enough to divorce her emotions from the sex. That was all it was. A totally natural chemical response to what had happened.

She stood up again and ignored the fact that she still felt a little shaky. As if she hadn't entirely convinced herself.

Dax had to be here somewhere.

After searching the media room and the pool, and still with no sign of Dax, Laia decided to put together a little brunch picnic and go down to the beach where she'd found him the other day.

When she emerged from the treeline she saw him straight away. He was sitting near the shoreline with his knees drawn up. His hair was wet—he'd obviously been swimming—and was wearing a pair of short swim trunks.

Laia was momentarily mesmerised by all that gleaming dark olive skin and muscle definition. She'd felt the awesome power in his body last night, and had a sense of how much it had taken for him to maintain control and be gentle with her.

As if sensing her behind him, he turned his head. She left the basket she'd brought under the trees, in the shade, and walked towards him.

She stood beside him, glad of the sunhat she wore. The hurt she'd felt that he'd not waited for her or made her breakfast still stung.

She pushed it away.

'Here you are,' she said.

'You sounded busy.'

Laia frowned. 'You heard me?'

Dax's jaw clenched. He said, 'Don't worry, it wasn't audible.'

Laia sank down beside him, guilt resurfacing. 'You tried the door, didn't you?'

'I tested it, yes.'

Laia felt something very delicate unfurling inside her as she took in his tense demeanour. He was hurt.

Because she'd shut him out.

'Dax, I did it without thinking. Not because I don't trust you. The truth is that I was talking to one of my advisors about travelling back to Isla'Rosa, making arrangements.'

Dax smiled, but it was tight, humourless. 'You've won—got your way. There will be no marriage.'

'Not between me and your brother. No.'

He looked at her. 'So there's no real reason for me to stay here now, is there? Would you stop me leaving?'

Laia's gut turned to stone. She knew what she had to say.

'No, there's no real reason for you to stay. Or me. Even if you told Aristedes where I am, there's not much he can do about it now. If you want to leave, Dax, you can. But…' She stalled.

Laia was ashamed to admit she was suddenly terrified. Terrified of what she wanted to ask and terrified of what Dax would do. This was his perfect opportunity to wreak revenge on her for having upended his life.

That cold blue gaze was so different from last night,

when it had burned her alive. Laia shivered in spite of the heat.

He raised a brow. 'But...?'

Laia dared herself to be vulnerable. 'But I would like you to stay...until we have to leave.'

'To do what, exactly?'

Laia's insides dropped. He was angry, and he was wreaking his revenge, and she couldn't blame him. He would walk away from her now...leave her behind.

For the first time in her life Laia realised that she'd protected herself from this kind of pain by not forming close relationships. Deep down she'd always feared rejection or abandonment, because of her mother's untimely death.

Her half-sister Maddi was the only person she'd allowed herself to get close to, and it had taken her years to build up the courage to go and find her.

In that moment Laia felt absurdly emotional...as if she'd ruined something. She didn't get emotional. She'd learnt at an early age to hide her emotions.

Her father had used to say to her, *'You can cry in private, Laia, but no one wants to see their King or Queen be weak in public.'*

Terrified Dax would see the tears pricking her eyes, Laia got up and said, 'It's fine. Forget it, Dax. If you want to go I won't stop you.'

She turned and went back up the beach, but after a couple of seconds she heard a muffled curse behind her and Dax caught her arm, stopping her.

He came around and stood in front of her. Laia looked down. He tipped up her chin. She couldn't hide her emotion. He cursed again.

He said, 'I know it's ridiculous, but after last night… that locked door was like a slap in the face. I'm not your enemy, Laia.'

No. He was something she didn't even want to investigate.

Laia blinked back the emotion. Her chest felt very full. 'I know that. It was a reflex. To be fair, it's not as if I have all my doors open at the castle and people coming in and out as they please.'

He looked slightly horrified. 'I should hope not. That would put your safety and security at risk.'

The thought of having someone like Dax caring about her safety and security made Laia feel wobbly all over again.

'Do you want me to stay, Laia?' Dax asked.

She felt as if she was on the verge of a cliff, with nothing to stop her freefalling over the edge.

She nodded. 'Yes, but only if you want to.'

Dax cupped her jaw, a thumb moving across her cheek. 'I want to. How long have we got?'

Laia had to ignore the dart of resentment that this was finite. That she had been born to a life of duty and responsibility.

'Twenty-four hours…'

Dax smiled, and it was sexy and wicked. The tension was gone as if it had never been there.

'Now you have me here for a whole twenty-four hours, what will you do with me?'

Laia fell over the edge of the cliff. It was a dizzying, soaring, swooping feeling of letting go all the shackles that bound her to everything she knew. Dax was here of his own free will. Because he wanted to be. Because he wanted to spend time with her.

But underlying it were a thousand voices urging her to be careful. What was she doing? What was she risking by indulging so selfishly like this?

She ignored them all. Pushed them away. Embraced her finite freedom.

Twenty-four measly hours. That was all she was asking for.

She couldn't help smiling. 'First, we eat. I brought a picnic.'

'So, how many languages do you speak?' Laia asked Dax.

Dax was leaning on his bent arm, long legs stretched out and crossed at the ankle. They were under the shade of the trees, eating the picnic Laia had prepared.

Laia was trying not to ogle his body. He looked up to the sky and squinted a little as he mentally calculated, and then he looked at her and said, 'Seven.'

Laia's mouth dropped open. 'Seven? I only speak five.'

'Which five?' Dax popped a grape into his mouth.

Laia ticked off her fingers. 'French, Spanish, German, Italian and English, of course.'

'Oh, well, if we're counting English then I've got eight.'

Laia sat cross-legged on the sand. 'Okay, come on. Let's have them.'

Now Dax ticked off his fingers. 'English, Spanish, French, Italian, German, Mandarin, Russian and Arabic.'

Laia made a whistling sound. 'That's impressive.'

Dax shrugged. 'I'm able to pick up languages very easily. I learn aurally. Make me write something down, though, and it'd be a disaster.'

'Because of your dyslexia?'

Dax nodded.

'Still, diplomatically you must go down a storm if you can converse with everyone.'

'It does go well in meetings—especially when people don't think I can understand what they're saying.'

Laia could imagine people assuming Dax was all fluff and no substance.

She squinted at him. 'Are you ever going to let people see the astute global businessman?'

He made a face. 'I'm running out of people to surprise, so I might have to.'

Laia laughed.

Dax looked at her mouth.

The air crackled between them.

Laia hadn't realised how long they'd been sitting under the trees, eating and drinking sparkling wine. She'd felt deliciously relaxed, and yet now, with Dax's gaze on her mouth, she felt energised again.

She hadn't taken her kaftan off, and she suddenly felt the heat of the day. 'I might go for a quick dip to cool down.'

Dax stood up in an impressively fluid motion. He held out his hand. 'I'll come too. But we've just eaten so we should be careful.'

Another little piece of Laia's heart tightened. This man was so considerate. How had he ever managed to persuade people he was a feckless playboy?

He stepped towards her and bent to grab the edges of her kaftan, pulling it up. 'But first we leave this behind.'

It was up and off, over Laia's head and on the sand behind her, before she knew what was happening, and Dax's gaze made a slow perusal of her body in the skimpy white bikini.

This is how he got his reputation, a little voice pointed out.

Because he could look at a woman like this and turn her into a puddle of desire without even touching her. No wonder so many of his lovers had felt compelled to spill their guts about their time with him.

'Why are you scowling?'

Laia realised Dax was looking at her face. She rearranged her features. She wasn't about to tell him she was madly jealous.

'No reason. Let's go.'

He took her hand again and they walked to the water. Just before she could put a toe into the gently foaming waves Laia squealed, as the world was upended and Dax lifted her over his shoulder, striding into the sea.

She didn't even bother protesting. She was enjoying the view of his muscular buttocks too much. She pushed aside all maddening thoughts of other women aside. She was here with him now, and he was staying because he wanted to. That was all that mattered.

Dax was lying on the sarong that Laia had brought down to the beach. They were drying off in the sun, near the shore.

His stomach still hurt from laughing at Laia's indignant face after her dunking.

She'd actually said, 'You do realise I'm about to be crowned Queen?' And so he'd dunked her again.

He said now, 'I can't remember the last time I laughed that much.'

Laia huffed. 'You're easily pleased.'

Dax came up on an elbow and looked down at Laia. Her eyes were closed. Lashes long and dark on her cheeks. Her skin had taken on a deeper golden glow. That bikini needed to come with a health warning. It barely covered the firm swells of her breasts.

Her eyes opened and Dax looked away.

She squinted up at him. 'When *was* the last time you laughed like that?'

It hadn't been with a woman. No woman had ever made him laugh. He knew when, and it made him melancholic. 'With Ari...when we were kids. Before he had to start going to his lessons.'

Dax put his hand on Laia's flat belly, spreading his fingers out, revelling in the way her muscles quivered a little under his touch.

Laia came up on her elbow now, and Dax's hand moved to the dip in her waist. 'What happened with your mother?'

To his surprise, Dax didn't automatically feel like shutting down her question. It was as if something had been defused inside him.

He squeezed Laia's waist gently, and then said, 'What *didn't* happen is the question.'

Laia's eyes filled with emotion. 'If you don't want to talk about it...'

Dax had never spoken about this to anyone. The only other person who knew was Ari, and even he didn't know everything. Because Dax had kept it from him, not wanting to burden him.

'She was a broken woman. In emotional pain. She felt trapped… She probably could have left and moved on. But she didn't. She was too proud. So she hid the pain, or thought she hid it, by taking pills. By drinking. By eating and purging.'

Laia touched the tattoo of the caged bird on Dax's chest. 'This is about your mother, isn't it?'

Dax's jaw clenched. 'Love is a trap. It cages you. It caged her. It caged your father…he never moved on.'

'I never saw it like that, but you're right. He tried to move on with the affair, but the guilt of it caged him for the rest of his life.'

Laia took her hand away from Dax's chest. 'Your mother depended on you, didn't she? Too much.'

Dax didn't answer for a long moment, and then he took his hand off her waist and sat up, drawing his knees up. He looked out to sea.

'I was the only one close enough that she *could* talk to. Ari was busy. Her husband was taunting her…she had no close girlfriends or family. She was lonely.'

Laia sat up too, curling her legs under her. 'You were very young to be taken into her confidence like that. She was the adult.'

'Most of the time I felt like the adult. I was even putting her to bed at night.'

'Dax…'

'The day of the crash…she was really out of it. But

she wanted to go out. Insisted. I only went with her because she refused to listen to me. I was worried.'

Laia spoke carefully. 'You weren't driving the car,
were you? *She* was…'

CHAPTER NINE

A MUSCLE PULSED in Dax's jaw. He looked at Laia and she nearly gasped out loud. There was so much pain in his eyes. Pain and...*guilt.*

He said, 'I did everything I could, but she wouldn't listen. And she wouldn't let me drive, even though I knew how. I might not have been legal, but I would have been safer than her. She took a corner too fast and we went straight off the road into a ravine... I had barely a scratch on me. A broken wrist. That was it.'

Laia felt cold. 'She could have taken you all the way down with her.'

Dax said nothing for a long moment, and then, 'In a way she did.'

Laia thought of something. 'The other night you were saying that you didn't deserve me...or this... You really believe you don't deserve what...? For someone to want you?'

Dax tensed visibly. 'Because it's my fault. I didn't help her. I watched her self-destruct. I let it happen. And then I turned my back on Santanger and a life of duty. I don't believe I deserve good things. Just like I don't deserve to be protected. I won't have a security team because I won't let anyone risk their life for me.'

Laia's heart ached at Dax's pain and palpable guilt. At the thought that he wouldn't put anyone at risk because of him.

She said, 'You know, we have something in common.'

He looked at her. 'We do?'

She nodded. 'I blame myself for my mother's death too. Even though I know it's not rational. But if I wasn't here…she would still be alive.'

'And you wouldn't be here.' Dax shook his head, 'You can't possibly think like that.'

'Your guilt and sense of responsibility isn't rational either.'

'Isn't it?'

'Why did you take the blame for the crash?'

'Because I wanted to protect her reputation. It was all she had. Her pride. No one outside of the palace knew how bad she was.'

No wonder he'd abdicated so much of his other responsibilities—he'd been crushed under the weight of this one.

'It wasn't your responsibility.'

He looked at her. 'Wasn't it?'

Laia shook her head. 'No, it wasn't. But you did it because you loved her and wanted to protect her.'

And now he didn't believe in love.

For a moment it was as if the sun had gone behind a cloud, even though there wasn't a cloud in the sky. Dax reached for Laia, putting his hands on her waist and laying down, pulling her over him.

Her salty damp hair fell around them in a tangle. Her skin felt sandblasted. She was pressed against him, every inch. And she suddenly wanted him again with a hunger that rose up like a wildfire.

Her hands were splayed on his chest. Over that tattoo. She covered it with her fingers. She didn't want to think about that now. He caught her hair and moved it over one shoulder, wound it around his hand, tugging her head down to his.

Something silent moved between them.

Enough talking.

Laia needed no further encouragement to lower her head to Dax's and cover his mouth with hers. At first she was tentative, shy. Dax was under her, all that power and strength, and she felt self-conscious. Aware that she couldn't possibly be as alluring as his other lovers.

But then she felt him smile against her mouth, and she put her hands around his face and kissed him with all the pent-up emotion he was causing within her, simultaneously hating him for not just being the Playboy Prince and feeling a multitude of complicated emotions for the man he actually was.

Dax quickly took control, flipping them so that Laia was under him, one of his thighs between hers. His body was stirring against her. She moved against him. He shook his head. She pouted. He laughed.

'We are not making love here. We have no protection.'

Laia cursed her lack of foresight. Dax stood up and took her hand, pulling her up. They gathered up the picnic detritus and made their way back to the villa.

Dax took the picnic things from Laia and put them

down on the kitchen table, then led her up to his suite, where he took her into the bathroom. He turned on the shower, which was open to the elements, and steam drifted upwards and all around them.

He took off Laia's kaftan again and turned her around, undoing her bikini and peeling it away. He stepped out of his own shorts. Laia marvelled that she didn't feel more self-conscious—but how could she when he was in front of her, naked?

There was something very elemental about being in this place, surrounded by heat and lush forest. Just them.

Dax stepped under the shower, bringing Laia with him. He washed her hair, working it into a lather and then massaging her skull with strong hands. Laia's head fell back at the exquisiteness of his touch. Then he rinsed her hair and worked soap into his hands again, to wash her body so thoroughly that she was shaking when his hand slipped between her legs and he found where she was so slick and ready.

It only took the barest of touches for her to come apart against his hand. She would have fallen at his feet if he hadn't held her up. She couldn't speak. She could only be manoeuvred as he turned off the shower and dried her hair, wrapped her in a towel.

He knotted a towel around his own waist. Laia looked at him, and this time she took him by the hand and led him into the bedroom. She wanted to worship at this man's feet.

She undid the towel at his waist she bent down in front of his majestic masculinity.

Roughly, he said, 'Laia, you don't have to…'

But Laia ignored him and wrapped her hand around

him, in awe at the vulnerability and the strength of him. She felt powerful at Dax's feet in a way that only he had evoked within her. Powerful in her newfound sensuality and femininity.

She bent forward and experimented, flicking her tongue over the head of his erection. A shudder went through his body and she felt it all the way down to her own core, where she was still slick, aching for more. Her breasts felt tight.

Laia took more of him into her mouth, exploring the thick, hard, shaft of flesh. She heard an indrawn hiss of breath, felt the tension in Dax's body, and the way his hips started to move.

But then he reached down and pulled her up. His cheeks were slashed with colour, eyes blazing. Hot again. Not cold.

'I need to be inside you *now*.'

Laia lay back on the bed and Dax came over her, entering her body in a smooth thrust so deep and all-consuming that she arched against him. But then he cursed and withdrew, and Laia let out a little cry. It had felt so good…skin on skin.

And then she saw him roll protection onto his length. *Oh*.

Heat suffused her whole body. She hadn't even thought about protection.

He came back and smoothed a hand up her thigh to her breast. He cupped the flesh and bent his head, surrounding one nipple in hot, wet heat just as he entered her again. Laia threw her head back and gritted her jaw, as if that might help contain the building tension coiling deep inside her, stoked by Dax's body moving in and out in a rhythm that made her feverish for release.

But he kept her on the brink…a form of delicious torture…until Laia could stand it no more and cried out, begging, pleading for him to let her go.

And finally, having mercy, he did. He thrust so deep and hard that he stole every coherent thought in Laia's head. She was no longer human. She was energy and light and an immense pleasure that gripped Dax tight, deep within her body, as he found his own release and shouted out. And then they both tumbled and fell back to earth.

Dax stood on the deck outside the bedroom. It was dusk, but the sky wasn't lavender—it was grey and threatening. The air felt heavy and full of pent-up electricity. A storm was coming. He could see the fishing boats heading back for the bigger island. He noticed that even the security team's boat had moved, presumably to a more sheltered area.

But even though the atmosphere was heavy, for the first time in a long time Dax felt light. Lighter. As if a burden had been lifted.

Talking to Laia…telling her about his mother…the crash…had been cathartic. Laia's calm and compassionate acceptance of what he'd said—the ugliness he'd held inside him for so long—had been like a balm.

Maybe he was finally letting go of the crushing guilt that should never have been his to bear. Maybe he'd finally feel worthy.

Dax turned around. The net was around the bed, so he couldn't see Laia, but he could imagine her. Naked.

Limbs sprawled in glorious abandon. The dips and hollows, the firm swells of her buttocks and breasts. Those eyes that opened wide when he joined their bodies and the way she had knelt at his feet like the most decadent supplicant. She'd tortured him a little. She was learning fast.

And soon she won't be yours any more. You've initiated her for someone else. Someone she can love and respect.

The thought of Laia moving on and finding this man who would be worthy of her love and respect was enough to make bile form in Dax's belly. He cursed himself and turned around again, putting his hands on the railing.

What the hell did he want? To keep seeing Laia beyond this point?

Yes. The answer was emphatic.

But it was impossible. She would be crowned Queen within days and her life would not be her own. She would be watched and commented on. If Dax went near her it would cause a sensation and a ream of headlines about his suitability.

He was not her destiny. She was not his. He had lived a life that put him firmly in the very *un*suitable bracket for a queen. He could never be a king. He'd learnt that a long time ago.

He heard a squeal from behind him and turned around to see Laia in a robe, belting it at her waist. She looked so beautiful it hurt. She was grinning.

'A storm! We have to close all the doors and shutters downstairs!'

Dax welcomed the distraction, he hadn't even noticed

that it had started to rain. He told himself he must be losing it. This tropical island paradise and the best sex he'd ever had were a potent combination for inducing crazy thoughts. Not real. Crazy.

Dax followed as Laia ran downstairs and started to pull the shutters and heavy blinds closed against the rain that was quickly turning torrential. He did the same on the other side of the room.

They met in the middle, and as soon as the room was protected against the rain he took her lapels in his hands and pulled her towards him. She went willingly, cleaving against him in a way that made his blood hum.

He smiled. 'You like storms?'

'I love them. They're so…awe-inspiring. Especially here. It feels like the world is ending, but it'll blow over in a few hours.'

It was almost as dark as night now. The storm was creating an otherworldly atmosphere. Dax had never particularly liked storms—too reminiscent of the emotional storms of his childhood. But this one was okay.

Because of Laia.

Impulsively he said, 'I'd like to take you out to dinner.'

Laia went very still. Did he actually mean take her *out* for dinner? In the real world? Where there were other people and regular restaurants and…?

It couldn't happen.

Laia imagined a scenario where she was out with Dax and the immediate frenzy of press attention.

'Dax… I don't know if that's—'

'I don't mean out there.' He jerked his head sideways

to indicate beyond the villa. This island. This bubble. 'I meant here. Now. I hear there's a fabulous restaurant called La Permata? Maybe you've heard of it?'

Laia was surprised by the strength of the disappointment she felt. But she forced a smile. This could not extend beyond the island. They both knew that. Time was slipping away from them like sand in a glass. This time tomorrow they wouldn't even—

She shut that line of thought down and put her head on one side and pretended to consider. 'I think I've heard of it… It's renowned for its eclectic menu and the novelty factor of using amateur chefs.'

'The very one. So, will you? Come to dinner with me?'

Laia's heart beat fast. 'What's the dress code?'

Dax looked affronted. 'Why, black tie, of course.'

Laia's heart thumped even faster at this side of Dax. Romantic.

She said, 'Then, yes, I would love to accept your invitation.'

Later that evening the storm had passed, as Laia had predicted. The sky was clear again, stars twinkling. There was a delicious feeling of freshness in the air and the earth smelled damp and rich from the rain. The heat wasn't as oppressive.

Laia was in her own bedroom. She'd showered and was in a robe looking for a dress. *Black tie.* It was ridiculous, really. But all Laia could think about right now was that memory of meeting Dax for the first time. When she'd been sixteen and had felt so gauche and fussy.

She realised she was living out the fantasy she'd harboured since that day. Since she'd looked at all those pictures of him with beautiful woman after beautiful woman.

She went into the dressing room and almost immediately a shimmering blue-green material caught her eye. She pulled it out. It was a maxi-dress. The simplicity of it appealed to her. It was backless. There was a silken ribbon that tied around her neck, holding the dress up, the ends trailing down her bare back. It fell in a swathe of greens and blues and teal colours down to her feet and it shimmered when she moved.

She hadn't worn jewellery since being on the island, but now she picked out some gold hoops for her ears and a gold bangle that sat on her upper arm. A gold signet ring for her little finger.

She pulled her hair back and up into a messy bun, leaving tendrils down around her face. She put on some make-up—only enough to take away the naked look. A dusting of green and gold eyeshadow. She didn't need blusher. Just thinking about the last few hours spent in bed made her blush. Some powder. A slick of flesh-coloured lipstick. Eyeliner and mascara.

She looked at herself in the mirror. After not wearing make-up for days, she felt like a clown. Did she measure up to the other women that Dax had been with? She hated this insecure, needy side of herself. But maybe this was what a passionate relationship did to you?

There was a knock on the door. 'Ready when you are.'

Laia called out, 'Okay…' but it sounded husky.

She turned away from the mirror. Slipped her feet

into high-heeled sandals. She walked to the door feeling like a foal standing on its legs for the first time.

The dress moved against her body like a silken whisper, heightening her sensitivity. The only underwear she wore was knickers.

She opened her door and nearly fell backwards. Dax was standing in the corridor in a classic black tuxedo. Hair still damp. Jaw clean-shaven. It made him look no less dangerous or decadent.

His gaze moved up and down her body, and when he looked into her eyes she knew she'd never feel more beautiful than she did in this moment. He looked *awed*.

'You are stunning, Laia.'

It was hard to find her voice. 'Thank you, so are you.'

He dipped his head. 'Thank you.' He held out his arm. 'May I escort you?'

Laia slipped her arm into his, and all that heat and steely strength immediately made her feel protected.

A thought ran through her mind. *How was she going to cope without him?* She wasn't his to protect. Life as a queen's consort? He'd rejected the life of a royal a long time ago. And who could blame him?

Dax led her downstairs, oblivious to her thoughts in turmoil. But when they reached the bottom of the stairs everything in her mind blanked. The villa had surely been dressed by a set decorator?

Candles were alight everywhere. There were vases of flowers. Dax must have gone out in the dusk after the storm and picked them from the rain-laden bushes. The dinner table was on the terrace outside, with a white tablecloth and silver settings, more flowers and crystal glasses. And another candle.

Laia was breathless. She let Dax's arm go and moved into the kitchen. There was a delicious aroma of cooking...

She wrinkled her nose and looked at Dax in a bid to try and avoid thinking about all the effort he'd gone to. 'Chicken?'

'Wait and see.'

He had a bottle of champagne in an ice bucket and took it out and opened it, pouring the sparkling effervescent wine into a tall flute, handing it to her before pouring his own.

Laia waited, and when he had his she said, 'Dax, this all looks...amazing. Thank you.'

He clinked his glass against hers. 'You haven't eaten yet...reserve your judgement.'

But she already knew it would be amazing. The best meal of her life.

She took a sip of wine and said, 'I have to admit something.'

Dax said, 'Go on.'

'This is my first date. Like, my first *proper* date.'

A funny expression came over his face, but it was gone before she could decipher it. He put his hand on her waist and tugged her closer. She felt her dress moving over her bare skin.

He slipped his arm around her, his hand touching the bare skin of her back. 'Well, then,' he said, 'I'm honoured to be your first date.'

The moment and the feel of his hand on her back, now making small movements over her skin, made Laia want to melt. But not now.

Later. She pulled back a bit and said, 'Do you need help with the food?'

Dax took her hand and led her over to the table, pulling out a chair so she could sit down. He said, 'You are not to lift a finger.'

He went back to the kitchen and Laia put her chin on her hand and just watched him. He put on some music. Soft and jazzy. Perfect. And after a few minutes he brought over the plates.

He put one down in front of Laia and said, 'Chicken satay in a peanut sauce and some mezze dishes.'

It looked mouthwatering. There was houmous and pitta bread, rice balls infused with herbs, feta cheese and salad... She took a taste of the chicken and it was so tender it melted on her tongue, the peanut sauce giving it a tangy and very Malaysian twist.

They ate in companionable silence for a few minutes, and then Dax took a sip of wine and sat back. 'Tell me something about yourself.'

'Like what?' Laia felt deliciously sated. From the wine...the food...*the sex*. This place. The calls of the night insects. The soft breeze bringing tropical scents.

Dax shrugged. 'I don't know... Anything. A secret. Something other people don't know.'

Laia thought for a second and then said, a little sheepishly, 'I'm terrified of dogs.'

Dax looked at her. 'Dogs?'

Laia nodded. 'But the embarrassing thing is that it's not really my fear.'

'What do you mean?'

'My father was attacked as a child by a stray dog. He never got over the fear and passed it down to me.

But I hate my fear. I'd like to have a dog. A puppy. But I can't do it. I always loved the idea of a family dog. A big shaggy thing that's goofy and silly. But if I even saw such a dog in the street I'd be rigid with fear.'

'You're brave, Laia. You'll get over that fear.'

'You think I'm brave?' Laia's insides fizzed a little.

'You stood your ground against an archaic agreement made by men and went your own way.'

'I don't know…it doesn't feel very brave to have been avoiding King Aristedes like this.'

'You're right, though, he wouldn't have listened. He would have done all he could to persuade you that you had to do the right thing. Because it would have suited *him*. We come from the same place. After what we saw, we're programmed to steer clear of emotional entanglement and drama. But, he would have been a kind and respectful husband.'

Steer clear of emotional entanglement.

That summed up Dax's attitude to relationships. She wondered if this counted as an emotional entanglement and then chastised herself. This was just sex. For him. For her…? She feared she was already way out of her depth.

But while they were here she could pretend that she wouldn't have to face the consequences of her actions.

She said softly, 'Do we have to leave here? Couldn't we just stay and pretend that the real world isn't out there, waiting?'

'We could…if you didn't have to be crowned Queen of Isla'Rosa and if I didn't have a business to run.'

Dax's easy acknowledgement that they would be

leaving told her in no uncertain terms that he was already moving on.

Laia thought of all that awaited her once she left this place. She realised she didn't want to do it on her own.

She wanted Dax by her side.

That realisation lodged in her gut and in her heart like a stone.

No. She told herself. It was just sex. Messing with her head. She wasn't experienced. She was adding emotion to sex and coming up with the wrong number.

To prove to herself that it was just sex, Laia got up and held out a hand to Dax. He looked at her with those bright blue eyes. Bright enough to sear her alive.

He arched a brow. 'No dessert?'

'I'm dessert.' She smiled, but it felt hollow.

He took her hand and stood up, and Laia led him from the beautifully decorated room up the stairs to the bedroom. In the soft golden light he took off his clothes, and Laia took off all her jewellery and laid it down. She undid the ribbon at the back of her neck that held the dress up. Took off her underwear.

They were both naked.

Dax let her hair down. And then he led her to the bed. He lay down, urging her to sit astride him. Laia spread her legs either side of his hips and came down over his chest, her breasts crushed against him. He lay under her, looking stubbled and dark and thoroughly decadent.

For now, for this short time, he was hers. And she would store away these moments deep down and carry them with her through the next weeks, months and years, while she lived her life of duty with someone by her side who would love her and respect her and cherish her.

But she already knew, fatally, that they would never make her *want* like this again.

As if reading her thoughts, Dax put his hands on her waist and shifted her slightly. 'Sit up…put your hands on my chest.'

She did. Dax looked at her with such heat and desire in his eyes and his expression that Laia wanted to take a mental screenshot. He cupped her breasts, rubbing his thumbs back and forth over her nipples, making her shiver. Her hips felt restless. She wanted him. Deep inside. He put his hands back on her waist again and encouraged her to come up, before bringing her back down onto his hard body.

Laia's head fell back at the sensation. She sat for a long moment, savouring the feeling of his body in hers. And then she started to move in an instinctive dance, watching as his control started to fray and come apart at the seams. He was holding her, sweat on his brow, begging her to let him move under her, but she didn't allow it. She felt merciless as she punished him for ruining her for all other men, and it was only when he lost it under her that she allowed herself to fall behind him, collapsing onto his chest.

It might be a victory, but it felt hollow.

'Dax, wake up…'

Dax cracked open an eye. Laia was hovering over him in a robe. Hair loose. It was still dark outside. His body felt heavy.

He lifted his head. 'Is something wrong?'

She shook her head and pulled back the cover. 'No, everything is fine. I just want to show you something. Put on a robe and a pair of shoes.'

Dax got up, wondering if he was still sleeping. He pulled on the robe that Laia held out and put on some sneakers. She took his hand and led him downstairs and out of the villa, switching on a powerful torch.

They were walking down the path that led to the beach when he stopped in his tracks. This wasn't a dream. The air was warm and very still around them.

'Laia…where are we going?'

She shone the torch in his face, momentarily blinding him. 'Just follow me and wait and see.'

He did as he was told, letting her lead him all the way down to the beach. It was a clear night, with the moon sending out a milky glow. They walked down close to the shore.

At first Dax saw nothing—then he did. A bluish light coming from the waves as they crashed to shore.

Laia, beside him, said, 'It's phosphorescence…a natural phenomenon.'

It was beautiful. 'I've heard of it, but I've never seen it.'

Laia put the torch down and started taking off her robe.

'What are you doing?'

She backed away towards the water. Naked. Gorgeous. 'Skinny-dipping. Come on!'

Dax didn't need any encouragement. He threw off the robe and followed Laia into the glowing water. A blissful contrast to the humid night. The water shimmered and glowed around them as they moved. It was magical.

They didn't go far from shore, just deep enough to go under water. Dax caught Laia by the legs and she came up spluttering and laughing. He felt an acute pain near his heart, knowing he'd never experience this again with her. But she might with someone else. With her children. He imagined bringing children to see this amazing spectacle. The excited squeals. Dark heads. A girl and a boy.

To drown out the pictures, he caught Laia to him. 'Wrap your legs around my waist.'

She did. And they were joined flesh to flesh. Breasts to chest. He kissed her there in the sea, under the moonlight in the glowing water, and for the first time in his life he found himself yearning for something he couldn't even name—because he'd never allowed himself to believe it could be possible.

Laia lay awake after they'd returned from the sea and made love. Again. There was a sick sense of dread pooling in her belly. The first fingers of dawn were evident in the sky outside.

It was time.

She could drag it out for another few hours. They could have breakfast together. Maybe even make love again. But it would be the desperate actions of a desperate woman.

A few hours ago in the water…the magical glowing water… Laia had known she was in love with Dax. A man who had told her in no uncertain terms that he had no interest in settling down. Having a family. And, after what he'd been through, she could understand it.

Dax could never be hers. All she could take would

be this experience. This knowledge he'd given her of herself as a sensual, desirable woman.

No man would ever make her feel the same. He'd ruined her years ago and he'd ruined her again. But this time fatally. Emotionally. And she'd let it happen. Invited it. Asked for it. *Begged*.

He moved minutely in the bed and Laia held her breath. When he didn't wake she let her eyes rove over his naked body. She'd known what it was like to lie with this man and have the freedom to touch him, to know he was hers. However briefly. But that was over now. She could never touch him again.

A sound of distress almost came out of her mouth. She had to put her hand up.

Before she could give in to the almost overwhelming temptation to touch him one last time, wake him with her body, Laia stole from the bed and went back to her own room.

She didn't look back. She couldn't. Because she knew that if she did she'd imprison them both here forever, and that was a fantasy that could never come true.

CHAPTER TEN

WHEN DAX WOKE the next morning he wasn't sure what had woken him. He only knew that he was alone in bed. And he didn't like that.

Ironic after a lifetime of avoiding exactly that scenario.

Now he knew he wouldn't rest easy unless Laia was by his side and in his sight.

The previous night came back to him. The moonlit walk to the beach…the glowing water…

Coming back here, making love again and again. With a desperation that—

He sat up. They had to leave today.

Dax was filled with a sense of urgency. He needed to see Laia. *Now*. To talk to her. To say…

Dammit.

He didn't know what to say, but what he did know was that this couldn't be it. He had to see her again. Keep seeing her. In spite of the reasons why he shouldn't. Or couldn't.

Maybe she was making breakfast. Dax pulled on a pair of sweats and went downstairs, but even before he reached the kitchen he had the uneasy sense that he was alone.

It was another glorious day in paradise. But it didn't feel like paradise any more.

He saw a movement in his peripheral vision and a wave of relief went through him.

She hadn't left yet. She was on the main terrace.

But as he walked out and saw her fully, his sense of urgency faded and turned to wariness.

She turned to face him, and something turned to dust inside him. This was Laia, but not the Laia he'd had in bed last night, or in the phosphorescent sea. This was the Laia he'd met in Monaco, and when he'd first arrived here.

She was wearing a smart cream linen trouser suit. Silk chemise. Hair pulled back. Discreet jewellery.

Princess Laia, Queen-in-waiting. Ready to go back out into the world.

He felt exposed. Still a little fuzzy from sleep and an overload of pleasure. Dressed only in sweats.

He folded his arms across his chest. Retreated behind a wall. 'Going somewhere?'

For a second something flashed in her eyes, but then it was gone. 'You knew we only had another twenty-four hours. We can't leave together, in case we're seen. Shamil is on his way in the boat to pick you up. You'll be taken back to your hotel to get your things.'

She had it all worked out and organised.

Dax lifted his wrist and pretended to consult a non-existent watch. 'By my reckoning there are at least another three hours.'

Did he sound desperate? He felt desperate. And angry. That she was so put-together and not looking as if she was aching for him. As he was for her, even though his body was still heavy from the pleasure of their lovemaking.

He couldn't help saying, 'So that's it? You've had your secret passionate fling and now you're ready to embark on phase two of your life?'

Her cheeks flushed but it gave him no satisfaction.

'What else did you expect, Dax? Are you saying you want something more?'

He went very still. A sense of exposure prickled over his skin. Memories of his mother screeching and crying.

He said, 'Are you ready for this to be over?'

Now her eyes did flash. 'You know nothing else is possible. We can't have an affair. *I* can't have an affair.'

'Not with someone like me.'

She shook her head. She looked drawn all of a sudden. 'Even if I wanted to…we couldn't.'

Dax was tempted to say, *But you do want to?* But those toxic memories crowded his head again. The desperation he'd seen on his mother's face. He *wasn't* desperate. This was different. Infinitely different.

Laia said, 'I thought you would be happy to regain your freedom. Your life.'

It was ironic. He could now leave this island, but Dax knew that the last thing he'd feel was a sense of freedom. He saw over her shoulder that the security team's boat was approaching the pontoon. He also noticed belatedly that she had her suitcases lined up by her feet.

'You must have been up early.'

'I couldn't sleep.'

Yet Dax had slept. Like a baby. After a lifetime of insomnia.

'Dax... I...' She stalled. And then she said, 'I hope you're going to let people see the real you now.'

He looked at her. Eyes narrowed. 'What's that supposed to mean?'

'You're a good man, Dax, and you've been living a lie.'

Dios. This was even worse than he'd thought. She was trying to make him feel better. He welcomed a numbness building inside him.

'Believe me, I've enjoyed raising hell.'

'I'm sure. But isn't it time to move on from that life?'

'Settle down? Like you will?'

'I have no choice. It's my destiny. If I don't have children my line dies with me. That's hundreds of years of royal lineage.'

'I've already told you that's not what I'm interested in.'

'But...won't you be lonely? After all, Aristedes will be marrying too, having a family.'

'Like you, he has no choice. But I do. I've seen enough of family life to do me for a lifetime. The world doesn't need my genes passed down. Ari's are enough.'

As if to mock himself, Dax recalled the vision he'd had the previous night of children on the beach shrieking with excitement over the phosphorescence.

His sense of exposure went nuclear.

He could see the security men getting out of the boat in the distance. Presumably coming to get Laia and bring her luggage down.

He forced himself to look into her green eyes. 'Don't pity me in my lonely bachelor life, Laia. I'll be just fine.'

For a second she looked almost ill, but then she lifted her chin and said, 'I don't doubt you will, Dax.'

The security men arrived and wordlessly took Laia's luggage. She paused a moment before following them and said, 'Goodbye, Dax. I didn't expect for any of this to happen…but I'm glad it did. I'm glad to have got to know you.'

Was it his imagination or was her voice husky? And had her eyes been shimmering…?

Before Dax could wonder at that, and figure out what it meant, Laia was down on the beach. One of the security guards helped her up onto the pontoon by taking her hand, and for a second Dax saw red.

His hands were curled into fists at his sides. He only relaxed them when she was on the boat and sitting down. And then it was pulling away.

He could see the other boat arriving in the distance. Just as Laia had promised.

Now that she was no longer in front of him. Dax's gut swirled with emotions. He didn't want to think about how it had made him feel to hear her say, *'I hope you're going to let people see the real you now.'* The fact that he'd revealed more to her, here on this island, than to anyone else in his life was terrifying.

She'd called him a *good man*. Even though he'd all but propositioned her to have an affair. A woman who would be crowned Queen in a matter of days. A woman who deserved so much more than a tawdry affair with a playboy prince.

Every residual feeling of being unworthy and guilty swarmed up from his gut, reminding him of who he was and what he couldn't have. *Her.* And yet even now her voice came into his head. Telling him that he shouldn't feel guilty. That he deserved more.

He hadn't asked for that. He hadn't asked for any of this. And yet he knew that if someone told him right now that he could turn back time and erase the last week and a bit he would feel sick at the thought. Not to have known her? Not to have felt her moving under him? Over him? And not just the sex… The talking. Laughing. *Everything.*

'You're a gift,' she'd said to him.

Dax cursed out loud. A guttural curse. *Damn her.* He turned his back on the sight of her boat disappearing. On her. He was no gift to anyone and it was time for him to remember that. It was time to move on and get his life back on track.

Laia resolutely faced towards where she was going. Even though it killed her, she wouldn't look back at the island to try and catch a last glimpse of Dax. She'd just heard him confirm that there was no hope. He'd spelled it out clearly. Brutally.

'I've seen enough of family life to do me for a lifetime. The world doesn't need my genes passed down. Ari's are enough.'

All he was interested in was an affair. And he knew that wasn't possible. Not for her. It was time for her to be strong. She'd never needed to be stronger. Not even after her father's death. It was time to face her future and all that was ahead of her. The job of being Queen to her people.

And what about Laia the woman? asked a little voice.

She was afraid that Laia the woman had been left be-

hind on the island and she might never find her again.
From now on she was Queen first, woman second.

Two days later, Isla'Rosa

Laia was back at her desk in the castle in Sant'Rosa.
Somehow holding it together even though she felt as if
she was unravelling inside. Sometimes she wondered
if she'd dreamt the past ten days.

She'd arrived back a few hours before and had made
no comment about her upcoming nuptials, saying only
that she was preparing for the coronation.

She knew she had to try and figure out how to get
Maddi back—but at that moment the door to her office
burst open and, as if conjured out of her head, Maddi,
her half-sister, appeared.

Laia's insides dissolved into a pool of emotion. Relief and love.

'Maddi!'

They ran across the room and straight into each other's arms. Laia held on tight for a long moment, swal-
lowing down her emotion. Then she pulled back and
ran her hands all over her sister.

'Are you okay? Did Aristedes let you leave today or
did you have to escape?' She wasn't even aware of what
she was babbling.

Maddi stopped her. She said, 'Laia, it wasn't like
that. He found out almost straight away…but no one
else knew. I agreed to slot into the engagement schedule
because I thought that was the best way of letting you
stay hidden…if I was distracting him… But the truth
is—' Maddi broke off and walked away.

'Mads…?'

Her sister turned around. 'The truth is that I fell for him. We were…together.'

So she'd been right. 'I guess that was pretty apparent.'

Maddi frowned. 'What do you mean?'

Laia took her hand and led her over to an open laptop, where she'd been looking at the pictures of her and Aristedes.

Maddi blushed. Laia could sympathise. At least there were no pictures of her and Dax.

'I thought he was going to keep you on Santanger as some sort of a threat. That he wouldn't release you until I agreed to the marriage. But he let you go…'

Maddi's face turned to stone. 'Yes, he let me go.'

Maddi told Laia that Aristedes had come to terms with the fact that his marriage was off the table. That he'd realised he'd been complacent, expecting Laia to marry him.

'That's good. Did he say anything about the peace agreement?'

Maddi nodded. 'That you could discuss it at some point.'

'Maybe I didn't give him enough credit,' Laia said. *Just like his brother.*

Her conscience stung.

Maddi took her hands. 'What matters is that you're back in time for the coronation and there's nothing and no one to stop you becoming Queen.'

Laia immediately thought of Dax.

Maddi clearly saw her face. 'What is it? What are you not telling me? Did Ari's brother find you? Did something happen?'

Laia felt like crying and laughing all at once. He'd helped her find herself.

But she just shook her head. 'It's okay. I'll tell you about it later.'

Or never—because she wasn't sure she'd ever be able to articulate what had happened.

She said now, 'I'll draft a statement and send it over for Aristedes's approval. It will say that by mutual agreement we've decided not to marry. I hope he'll countersign.'

Maddi looked emotional. 'I'm sure he will. He's a good man, Laia. I think you'll like him when you do have your talks.'

Laia focused on Maddi to stop thinking about Dax, who was also a good man. She touched her sister's cheek. 'Oh, Mads, I'm sorry… Is there any hope…?'

Maddi shook her head. 'No, he made that clear. And it wasn't as if I didn't know.'

Laia said, 'Well, you're back where you belong. And I want everyone to know who you are—if you're ready?'

Up till now Maddi had been shying away from coming out as Laia's sister. As a princess.

But now Maddi nodded. 'Yes, I'm ready.'

Laia hugged her sister tight again. Then pulled back. 'I'm so happy, Mads. I'll need you by my side.'

They smiled at each other, but their smiles were distinctly wobbly.

The same day, Santanger

Dax was bleary-eyed and dishevelled in jeans and a shirt after the long transatlantic flight. He hadn't shaved since that morning. But he'd known where he had to come first. He was in the palace in Santanger, following the way to his brother's rooms without even thinking.

The guards let him into Ari's inner suite and Dax didn't even notice their wide-eyed looks at his appearance. He went in and stood at the inner doorway. His brother was on the other side of the room, drinking. A sight as *un*-Ari as anything he'd ever seen.

Suddenly Ari turned around with a look of such hope on his face that Dax knew it wasn't because he was expecting *him*.

His expression immediately closed off. 'Where the hell have you been?'

Dax went in and gestured to the glass in Ari's hand. 'Drinking before noon, Ari? Have you decided to join my gang?'

Dax heard himself saying the words, still perpetuating the myth of his infamy even now. He hadn't drunk before noon in years.

Laia's voice sounded in his head. *'You're a good man, Dax.'*

Dax drowned it out by pouring himself a shot of whisky and downing it.

'Dax…?'

Dax looked at his brother. 'I'm sorry, Ari.'

'For what?'

'For not bringing Laia back in time. We were… She has this island…in Malaysia. That's where we've been. I couldn't leave.'

He hated even having to tell his own brother where he'd been. It was as if he was betraying the memory.

And then Dax looked at his brother as a thought occurred to him.

What if he was going to still insist—?

'You know you can't marry her, right?'

'Yes, I know.'

Dax's tension levels dropped. He said, 'You'll find another princess.'

Then his brother said, 'What happened between you and Princess Laia?'

Dax felt guilty. It must have shown, because Ari said wearily, 'It's not as if I can't put two and two together, Dax. I had no real hold over her. It was an ancient agreement. I barely knew her.'

Dax looked at him. How could he explain the unexplainable. How she'd become the centre of his world? 'I tried not to, but...'

Ari asked, 'Did you know Laia was Maddi's sister?'

Dax sat down on a chair. Legs sprawled out. He nodded. 'But I couldn't get in touch with you. She threw my phone in the sea.'

To Dax's surprise, Ari let out a sharp laugh.

Dax leaned forward. 'What's so funny? This is a disaster.'

Ari wasn't laughing any more. And neither was Dax.

Two weeks later, Isla'Rosa

'So how do you feel, *Princess Maddi*?' Laia asked teasingly.

Maddi smiled shyly. 'I don't think I'll ever get used to it. Being a princess.'

They were walking through the grounds of the castle

in Sant'Rosa, enjoying the lull after the craziness of the coronation a week ago.

The world's press had descended on the small kingdom, lured by the pomp and the pageantry and the seismic announcement of a secret princess. Luckily, with the help of Laia's closest aide, Giorgio, it had all been handled with the utmost care and discretion, and after an initial flurry of headlines and shock the people of Isla'Rosa seemed to be coming around to the existence of Maddi.

She and Laia had done a small walkabout the day before, and the people hadn't been able to help but be charmed by their new Princess.

They hadn't held anything back about the King's affair. Maddi's mother had come back for the coronation, and she'd given an interview to one of Isla'Rosa's most respected newspapers. The people had sympathised with her heartbreak, and the outcome was not anger at the old King but a sense that he should have been brave enough to weather the storm to marry her.

'How are your mother and stepfather?'

Maddi smiled. 'They're good. It's been so lovely to see my mother here. Back in her home. They're already talking about moving here. Thank you for the house you've gifted them.'

Laia shook her head. 'Your mother deserves everything, Mads. She'll have whatever she wants for the rest of her life.'

She stopped when she saw tears in Maddi's eyes. 'Oh, Mads, I'm sorry—'

But Maddi shook her head. 'No, it's not that… Well,

it is…and I'm so happy that she's happy. But…' she trailed off.

Laia felt her own heart contract. She *knew*. Because she felt like crying too. 'It's him, isn't it? Aristedes?'

Maddi looked as if she wanted to deny it, but she nodded. Then she looked angry. 'I never asked to fall in love with him, but he made me… If I could go back there and give him a piece of my mind—'

'Why don't you?'

Maddi stopped and looked at Laia. Eyes wide. The same eyes, just darker. 'Go back and…what?'

Laia squeezed Maddi's hand. 'Tell him that you love him. What have you got to lose?'

Laia felt like a fraud. She hadn't had the courage to tell Dax how she felt. But she'd seen those pictures of Maddi and Aristedes. She was sure that they loved each other.

'What if he rejects me?'

He won't.

Laia would bet money on it. But she said lightly, 'Then you come back here, to your home, and we'll make an effigy and stick pins in his bottom.'

Maddi giggled. And then sobered. 'You're right. I need to do this.'

'So go and do it. Giorgio will help you get to him.'

Maddi looked alternately terrified and excited. She flung her arms around Laia's neck. 'I love you.'

Laia hugged her back, feeling emotional. She couldn't stop feeling emotional these days. She said, 'I love you too. Now *go*.'

Maddi left, walking quickly through the gardens.

Laia watched her go. Selfishly, she almost felt like

calling her back, because she knew that soon she'd be losing her sister again. But she said nothing. She went to the wall and looked out to sea and tried not to think about the person who dominated her every waking and sleeping moment.

Dax.

She put a hand on her belly. She'd been feeling queasy for a few days now. And she'd noticed that morning that her period was late. A trickle of fear traced down her spine, but she told herself she was being ridiculous. They'd never not been careful. It was undoubtedly due to the craziness of the last couple of weeks.

Every day she'd looked out at the people and the crowds and almost wished she would see a familiar tall, broad body amongst them. That beautiful face that could turn from serious to wicked to laughing in one instant.

But of course he wouldn't come after her. He wouldn't put her in that position. And he didn't want her enough. She'd already seen headlines saying that he was back in New York. And he'd been pictured at an event. Alone. She was thankful for that at least. She couldn't have borne seeing him with another woman so soon.

She couldn't be pregnant with Crown Prince Dax's baby. That would be the cruellest irony of all.

A month later, Santanger. Ari and Maddi's wedding

'I'd say your trip to Santanger to confront Aristedes was a success, wouldn't you?'

Maddi laughed and squeezed Laia's hand. She looked shy all of a sudden. 'I think we can say that, yes.'

The guests were mingling after the wedding reception in the beautiful ballroom at the Santanger palace. Guests spilled out through open French doors onto balconies and the sky was turning dusky. It was magical.

Laia felt emotional. *Again.*

'I'm so happy for you, Mads. Truly. You deserve everything the world has to offer—*Queen Maddi.*'

Maddi paled a little. 'I've only just been getting used to the idea of being a princess. This is ridiculous…'

Laia shook her head. 'You can do this. You're a natural.'

She spotted Aristedes coming over from the other side of the room and stood back. He winked at her and smiled as he took Maddi's hand to lead her away.

This marriage had already done so much for the two kingdoms. There had been some mutterings of dissent, but everyone was so happy to celebrate something joyful that they had been drowned out.

This really was a new era for Isla'Rosa and Santanger. Side by side. Just as Laia had wanted. It was a just pity that she was single-handedly going to ruin it all for everyone with a scandal. Any day now.

The ever-present queasiness was worse now. Much worse.

At that moment she spotted Dax across the room. As if she hadn't been aware of him, mouthwateringly sexy in his morning suit, for every second they'd shared the same air, during the wedding and the reception.

Somehow, miraculously, she'd managed to avoid coming into close proximity with him—no mean feat considering she was maid of honour and he was the best man.

Those blue eyes moved over the crowd and stopped on her. As if he'd been looking for her. She felt it like a jolt of electricity. Panic galvanised Laia. She simply could not come face to face with him. Not now. Not yet. She'd fall to pieces.

Her phone rang in her bag and she welcomed the distraction, taking it out. But when she heard what her advisor Giorgio was saying her legs nearly gave way.

The scandal was upon her.

She had to go. Leave now.

She found Maddi and told her she had to go, assuaging her concern by telling her it wasn't anything too serious, but serious enough that she had to return to Isla'Rosa.

She wouldn't ruin Maddi's happy day.

The news would come out soon enough.

Dax was staring at Laia so hard he was surprised she didn't have two holes in her forehead. Never in the history of weddings had the best man and maid of honour had less to do with one another.

For the life of him he couldn't seem to get across the room to her, where she was talking to Maddi. It was like a recurring dream, where he was following her but she kept disappearing. She'd turned avoiding him into a sport.

She was maddening. She was beautiful.

She wore a long, simple teal-coloured gown in the same style as the bride's very simple wedding dress. High-necked and long-sleeved, it was the epitome of classic elegance, but all Dax could see was that lithe body underneath. And was it his imagination or did she look even curvier?

Her hair was up and swept back in a smooth classic chignon. Her jewellery was discreet. The newly crowned Queen of Isla'Rosa was not putting a foor wrong.

Dax had watched her coronation on repeat for days. Obsessing over the fact that she looked pale. And serious. Who was supporting her? Caring for her? Protecting her?

She was obviously close to her sister, who'd been at her side throughout. He could be thankful for that. But he was also incredulous that Ari had been taken in by Maddi's subterfuge. To his mind they didn't look remotely alike.

He'd even lifted up his laptop one day and brought it into Ari. He'd pointed at the screen and said incredulously, 'Really, Ari? You really thought that *she*—' he'd stabbed at the screen over Maddi's face '—was *her*?' He stabbed at the screen over Laia's face.

Ari had just scowled at him, and soon afterwards Dax had left to go back to New York—where he'd alienated everyone around him with his bad mood. He'd even started to frequent Irish bars, seeking solace in their whiskey and their maudlin ten-verse songs about heartache and pain.

And now he was back in the eye of the storm. And Laia was ignoring him so determinedly it was a wonder her head didn't fall off.

He had to admit that his brother had never looked happier. And since when had he been a fan of public displays of affection? He couldn't keep his hands off his new wife. The new Queen of Santanger.

Ari had got his strategic marriage after all…and a woman he loved.

Dax had to admit to envy. Because what he wanted now was the same, but with the only woman who—

When Dax next looked for Laia she was gone.

Again.

Dammit.

He pushed through the crowd, determined to find her this time.

And say what? prompted a voice.

All Dax knew was that the thought of not seeing her, speaking to her…*touching her*…ever again was unconscionable. No matter what the consequences.

He finally made it to the other side of the ballroom and stepped out into the blessedly empty corridor. But there was no one. Nothing. Acrid disappointment filled his gut.

Then he saw a flash of dark green out of the corner of his eye. *Laia.*

Dax followed her. She wasn't going to escape again. He saw her then, walking fast towards an exit.

No way.

She'd stopped for a second, as if wondering which way to go, and Dax seized the opportunity. He'd caught up with her and said her name before she could move again.

He saw how she tensed and everything in him rejected it. Slowly she turned around. *Por Dios.* He'd missed her.

He shook his head. 'Laia, you've been avoiding me

for the whole day…what the hell is going on? Can't we even be civil with each other?'

Her face went red. A sign of life. Dax welcomed it.

She said. 'Of course. I didn't mean for it to be like this. But, look, I have to go back to Isla'Rosa. Something has come up. An emergency. A crisis.'

She turned around again and Dax caught her arm. She pulled away jerkily. Dax gritted his jaw against the hurt. She couldn't even bear to be touched by him.

He realised she looked very alone at that moment, and in spite of her obvious reluctance to be with him he felt protective. 'What's going on? Do you want me to come with you?'

She paled and backed away. 'No way. You are literally the last person I want to come with me right now.'

Dax felt winded. All he could do was watch as Laia started walking again. She went to the exit, where a car was waiting, and got into the back. He watched it pull away.

When Dax's brain started functioning again he wondered if he'd been deluded on the island. Had he really meant so little to her that she couldn't bear to be around him now? Did she regret everything in spite of what she'd said?

He wanted to turn away, leave and nurse his hurt. But something stopped him. Some instinct.

In spite of Laia's rejection she'd looked terrified. Something was going on.

Cursing himself for being such a sap, Dax got his things and arranged transport to Isla'Rosa.

When he arrived a couple of hours later he checked into a mid-range hotel, to draw less attention. Wearing a baseball cap, he left the hotel and walked around the capital city, Sant'Rosa. He was charmed by its quaint medieval streets, but he could see that it needed drastic modernisation and development.

He'd never been here before—it hadn't been considered necessary for him to visit when Ari had—and then Dax had wanted to put Santanger behind him. So Isla'Rosa had never really been on his radar.

The imposing castle stood on a hill overlooking the town. Not unlike the palace in Santanger, albeit on a much smaller scale. Laia was up there now. Dealing with whatever was going on.

Dax cursed himself for being an idiot and went back to the hotel, vowing to leave again first thing in the morning. Clearly she wanted nothing to do with him. She'd moved on.

But when he went out for coffee the following morning all he could see were huddles of people talking in whispers. Looking worried. He saw a newspaper stand and the picture of Laia on the front page caught his eyes.

He didn't even have to buy a copy to see the blazing headline, and when it sank in he realised what the crisis was.

And also that he wasn't leaving Isla'Rosa any time soon.

CHAPTER ELEVEN

One day later

LAIA SAT AT the head of a long boardroom table in the castle in Sant'Rosa. The capital city. But that was a bit of a stretch. It was more of a big town, with a lot of its medieval infrastructure still intact, which was lovely for the tourists but not so much for a modern economy.

Her head throbbed.

About twenty men looked at her with varying expressions of shock, dismay and disgust. There was only one of compassion. From her advisor Giorgio.

He'd called her with the news at the wedding reception. The news that was going to break all over Isla'Rosa's media. And it had. Yesterday. Luckily it didn't seem to have filtered through to Ari and Maddi on their honeymoon. *Yet*.

One of the men stood up at the end of the table. Laia vaguely recognised him as one of her father's less favoured advisors. She really had to do something about this motley crew.

He was shaking with agitation. 'Queen Laia, since no one else here seems prepared to say the unsayable, I must. How on earth is it possible that our virgin Queen is pregnant?'

Laia had the absurd urge to giggle, but Giorgio caught her eye and shook his head. She stood up. She needed to get more women into this room.

'Gentlemen. I know this comes as a huge shock, and believe me, I truly didn't plan—'

But she was quickly drowned out by a cacophony of voices. All the men were asking questions now, and predicting disaster and destruction.

One man's voice was more strident than everyone else's as he shouted out, 'Who on earth is the father? Is he even a royal?'

Before Laia could answer, the door at the end of the room swung open and a man appeared. Laia's legs wobbled so much she almost fell back into her chair. She locked her knees.

Dax stood there. In a three-piece suit. Shaved jaw. He'd even had a haircut. He hadn't looked this suave for his own brother's wedding.

He said, firmly and clearly, '*I* am the father of Queen Laia's baby. And, yes, I am royal. For anyone who doesn't recognise me, I'm Crown Prince Dax de Valle y Montero of Santanger.'

There were a few gasps around the table.

One of the men blustered, 'You can't just barge in here like this.'

Dax looked at Laia. This time there was no hiding. His blue gaze was mesmeric. She didn't want to look away. She felt tired. As if she'd been running for a long time.

He said, 'If you would all excuse us, please? I would like to talk to Queen Laia in private.'

One of the men gasped in outrage. 'You can't dismiss us.'

Laia didn't take her eyes off Dax. She was afraid if she did he'd disappear. She said, 'Please leave us.' And then, more softly, 'You too, Giorgio. I'll be fine.'

The men sidled out of the room with lots of mutterings and deep sighs. At last the door closed and they were alone. It was silent.

Dax walked towards her.

She said, 'What are you doing here? How did you know?'

He stopped a few feet away. 'I followed you back from Santanger, even though you'd made it clear I was the last person you wanted to see.'

Laia winced. 'Why?'

'Because I was worried about you.'

Laia's heart clenched. 'You've seen the newspapers?'

He nodded. 'I presume that is the crisis?'

She nodded. 'I hadn't been feeling well for the past month…a persistent queasiness.' She blushed. 'My period was late. Very late. I suspected what it was, but I was too terrified to get it confirmed. But eventually I had to go to the castle doctor, and he did a routine pregnancy test a couple of days ago. I think he was as shocked as me. One of his staff must have leaked it. Giorgio told me the media had the story the day before yesterday.'

Dax frowned. 'At the wedding—that's why you left?'

She nodded.

'But you already knew you were pregnant.'

Laia nodded. 'Only just. That's why I was avoiding you. I couldn't bear to look at you in case you saw... I was in shock. Trying to get my head around it. I felt so raw. If you'd come near me, touched me, I was afraid I'd combust or fall to pieces, and it was Maddi and Ari's celebration. I was terrified it would come out... somehow.'

'I thought you were avoiding me because you couldn't bear to look at me. Because you were ashamed of what had happened between us.'

Laia shook her head. She stepped out from the table and faced Dax. He came towards her and then stopped. Her hands itched to touch him. Feel him.

'Dax, I—'

But he closed the gap between them and put a finger to her mouth. Laia instinctively pressed a kiss against it. His eyes flared.

He took his finger away. 'I just have one thing I want to say.'

Laia swallowed. 'Okay...'

He cupped her face with his hands. 'I love you, Laia. I adore you. You changed my life on that island and I never want to return to being the person I was. Cynical and closed off and afraid to ask for *more*. Afraid to forgive myself. I'm sorry I didn't tell you this before I let you leave, but I was too scared to admit it.' He made a face. 'Okay, that was more than one thing. But I—'

This time Laia put a finger to his mouth. She smiled. She was coming apart inside, walls crumbling, hope rising, joy seeping into her blood and veins.

'I have a few things to say.'

She took her finger away. Dax said, 'Okay.'

'I love you too. I adore you. But I truly believed that you weren't interested in anything more. And I have to have more…because that's what is expected of me.'

Dax winced. 'I felt threatened when you asked me if I was going to let people see the real me. I hadn't realised until that moment how much I'd shared with you. You knew more than Ari. I'd never trusted anyone with so much. I knew deep down that I wanted you—and not just for an affair. But in that moment the thought of revealing that to you was…terrifying. Because I really believed you wouldn't choose me for a partner. Why would you? I have my reputation and all my baggage. You deserve someone far more worthy.'

Laia looked at his mouth. 'You are more than worthy, Dax. I don't want to ever leave you again. Please, kiss—'

She was in his arms and his mouth was on hers before she'd even finished speaking. It was bliss. She'd never thought she'd experience it again.

She pulled back, breathing hard. Dax's hair was messier now. Better.

She said, 'I've hated you for ruining me for all men.'

He smiled and it was wicked. 'Good. Because I've been hating you too—for being the only woman I want to have a life with that I never even wanted before. Now it's all I can think about.'

Laia shook her head. 'I don't really hate you. I love you, Dax.'

'I don't hate you either. I adore you.'

Dax led her over to the window seat and sat down, pulling her into his lap. Laia couldn't stop looking at him. Touching his face.

She said, 'You look so elegant.'

Dax blushed.

Laia laughed, joy bubbling up. 'What is it?'

'I knew I had to come here today and I wanted to make a good impression. I didn't want to give anyone an excuse to say I wasn't good enough.'

Laia put her hand on his cheek. He turned his head and pressed a kiss into her palm. She said, 'Oh, Dax, you're more than good enough.'

Then she bit her lip and brought his hand to her belly and its very delicate curve. 'We haven't even talked about this… How do you feel?'

'How do I feel?' Dax shook his head. 'I feel like bursting with pride. And happiness and joy. And I'm also terrified. Because my father was not a good role model, nor my mother… But with you, I want to be a father. That night when we went down to the sea…?'

Laia nodded. Her eyes were already pricking with tears.

'I imagined a family,' Dax continued. 'I imagined you with children, hearing their excitement. And I wanted to be part of that.'

Laia was crying in earnest now. 'I would love that.'

Dax put his hand over hers on her belly and said, 'Let's do it. Let's do it all together. For ever.'

Laia nodded and wrapped her arms around his neck. Dax's hands roved over her body, feeling every inch, relearning her shape. Making her blood grow hot. Making her want him. Right now.

She caught his tie, started to undo it. His hands were cupping her breasts, already fuller.

Then he said, 'Wait. I have to show you something.'

He pushed his tie aside and undid his shirt, pulling it open.

Laia looked—and sucked in a breath. There, high on his chest, near the tattoo of the caged bird, was another tattoo. Identical in style, except for the fact that in this tattoo the cage was open and the bird was flying free.

It was very new. Still raised and dark with ink. She touched it softly, reverently. Tears blurred her vision again. 'It's beautiful.'

There was a knock on the door. They looked at each other.

Laia called out, 'Two minutes.'

Dax gently put Laia off his lap and stood up. They rearranged themselves and Laia giggled. Then she sobered up for a second and said, 'Are you sure you're ready for this? You'll be the Queen's Consort. You might even have to walk a few feet behind me... I've always wanted to change that.'

Dax said, 'Slight issue, my love. You haven't agreed to marry me yet. But in theory I will walk ten feet behind you if I have to. That way I can look at your ass and make sure you're safe.'

Laia giggled again. Then she said, 'You'd better hurry up and ask me, then.'

Dax got down on one knee, and to her surprise took a box out of his pocket.

He said, 'This visit was only ending one way or I was never going to leave.' He looked up at her and said, 'My darling Laia Sant Roman, Queen of Isla'Rosa, will you please do me the honour of becoming my wife, mother of my firstborn child, and hopefully more?'

He opened the box and Laia gasped. It was a stunning emerald ring, glittering in a diamond and platinum setting. He took the ring out and held her hand, looked at her.

She looked back at him. 'What?'

'You haven't answered me yet.'

She moved down and bowled him backwards onto the floor, her arms wrapped around him. 'I thought that was obvious. Yes, yes, *yes!* I will marry you, Prince Dax. Now, can we please go somewhere and make love?'

Dax grinned and put the ring on Laia's finger, where it shone like the seas around Permata island.

A few minutes later they opened the door to Giorgio, who took a step back at the sight of their slightly dishevelled appearances.

Laia held up her hand with the ring and said, 'Can you organise a press conference? Say for tomorrow morning? And let's see how fast we can organise a royal wedding. And cancel all my meetings for the rest of the day and don't let anyone disturb us, okay?'

Giorgio nodded frantically, and then grinned, and he watched as the Queen of Isla'Rosa led her husband-to-be by the hand up to her private rooms.

EPILOGUE

Four years later, Permata

'PAPA, WHAT IS THAT? Is it magic?'

Dax looked at Laia in the moonlight and smiled. He turned his attention back to his daughter, Liselle, held high in his arms. They stood at the shoreline on the beach on Permata.

'No, it's not magic, but it looks like it, hmm? It's called bioluminescence, or phosphorescence.'

Their three-year-old daughter tried to repeat the word. 'Fozzi-essence?'

Dax chuckled. 'That's it.'

Liselle clapped her hands. 'Can I touch it?'

'Of course. Let's go into the water.'

Laia smiled as she watched her husband wade into the shallows holding Liselle by the hand. She was squealing with delight, exactly as Dax had envisaged.

And soon, when their son Demetriou started walking—which looked like any day now—he would join Liselle in the magic water. He was asleep on Laia's shoulder now, his sturdy body a welcome heavy weight.

Laia looked up to the moonlit sky in a bid to keep

back emotional tears. She had everything she'd ever dared to dream of and so much more. A man she loved who loved her. Endless passion. A family.

A growing family!

Maddi and Ari had just had twins, so now they had three children. Max, who was almost the same age as Liselle, and Tomas and Sara.

They hadn't been able to come on this trip, due to the twins' imminent birth, but Permata had become a private special haven for both families.

And Isla'Rosa was developing at a rate of knots—thanks to her clever husband. Much to Ari's chagrin, it was fast becoming one of Europe's biggest hubs for software development, keeping young people from emigrating and drawing people who wanted to live and work in a Mediterranean climate from all over the world.

The people of Isla'Rosa adored Dax, their King Consort. And the peace pact between Santanger and Isla'Rosa was a solid and enduring thing. Healing generations of hurt and pain.

Dax came back, holding Liselle. He put her down and reached for Demi, and Laia handed him over. Their little boy made a sound, but promptly fell back to sleep on his father's shoulder.

Dax took Laia's hand, and in her other hand she held her daughter's.

'Home?'

Laia nodded.

He saw her emotion and he kissed her. It was an acknowledgement and a promise of so much more to come.

She smiled. 'Yes, let's go home.'

* * * * *

Couldn't stop turning the pages of
Claimed by the Crown Prince*?*
*Then you're sure to fall in love with
the first installment in the*
Princess Brides for Royal Brothers *duet*
Mistaken as His Royal Bride

*And don't miss these other sensational
Abby Green stories!*

Bound by Her Shocking Secret
Their One-Night Rio Reunion
The Kiss She Claimed from the Greek
A Ring for the Spaniard's Revenge
His Housekeeper's Twin Baby Confession

Available now!

#4169 THE BABY HIS SECRETARY CARRIES
Bound by a Surrogate Baby
by Dani Collins

Faced with a hostile takeover, tycoon Gio must strengthen his claim on the Casella family company with a fake engagement. He'll never commit to a real one again. Despite his forbidden attraction, his dedicated PA, Molly, is ideal to play his adoring fiancée. The only problem? Molly's pregnant!

#4170 THE ITALIAN'S PREGNANT ENEMY
A Diamond in the Rough
by Maisey Yates

Billionaire Dario's electric night with his mentor's daughter Lyssia was already out-of-bounds. But six weeks later, she drops the bombshell that she's pregnant! Growing up on the streets of Rome, Dario fought for his safety, and he is determined to make his child equally safe. There is just one solution—marrying his enemy!

#4171 WEDDING NIGHT IN THE KING'S BED
by Caitlin Crews

Innocent Helene is unprepared for the wildfire that awakens at the sight of her convenient husband, King Gianluca San Felice. And she is undone by the craving that consumes them on their wedding night. But outside the royal bedchamber, Gianluca remains ice-cold—dare Helene believe their chemistry is enough to bring this powerful ruler to his knees?

#4172 THE BUMP IN THEIR FORBIDDEN REUNION
The Fast Track Billionaires' Club
by Amanda Cinelli

Former race car driver Grayson crashes Izzy's fertility appointment to reveal his late best friend's deceit before it's too late. He always desired Izzy, but their reunion unlocks something primal in Grayson. Knowing she feels it too compels the cynical billionaire to make a scandalous offer: *he'll* give her the family she wants!

#4173 HIS LAST-MINUTE DESERT QUEEN
by Annie West
Determined to save her cousin from an unwanted marriage, Miranda daringly kidnaps the groom-to-be, Sheikh Zamir. She didn't expect him to turn the tables and demand she become his queen instead—and now, he has all the power...

#4174 A VOW TO REDEEM THE GREEK
by Jackie Ashenden
The dying wish of Elena's adoptive father is to be reunited with his estranged son, Atticus. Whatever it takes, she must track down the reclusive billionaire. When she finally finds him, she's completely unprepared for the wildfire raging between them. Or for his father's unexpected demand that they marry!

#4175 AN INNOCENT'S DEAL WITH THE DEVIL
Billion-Dollar Fairy Tales
by Tara Pammi
When Yana Reddy's former stepbrother walks back into her life, his outrageous offer has her playing with fire! Nasir Hadeed will clear all her debts *if* she helps look after his daughter for three months. It's a dangerous deal—she's been burned by him before, and he remains the innocent's greatest temptation...

#4176 PLAYING THE SICILIAN'S GAME OF REVENGE
by Lorraine Hall
When Saverina Parisi discovers her engagement is part of fiancé Teo LaRosa's ruthless vendetta against her family's empire, her hurt is matched only by her need to destroy the same enemy. She'll play along and take pleasure in testing his patience. But Saverina doesn't expect their burning connection to evolve into so much more...

HPCNMRB1223